Prophet's End
and Other Stories

Scott D. Russell

Prophet's End Originally published by Dorrance Publishing Company, 2017.

Library of Congress Control Number: 2025903034
ISBN: 978-1-965733-41-7
12345678910
Written by Scott D. Russell.
Published by Stillwater River Publications, West Warwick, RI, USA.

Publisher's Cataloging-in-Publication
(Provided by Cassidy Cataloguing Services, Inc.)

Names: Russell, Scott D., 1945- author.
Title: Prophet's end and other stories / Scott D. Russell.
Description: [Second edition]. | First Stillwater River Publications edition. | West Warwick, RI, USA : Stillwater River Publications, [2025]
Identifiers: LCCN: 2025903034 | ISBN: 9781965733417 (paperback)
Subjects: LCSH: Hamill, Pete, 1935-2020--Fiction. | Bricker, Jen, 1987---Fiction. | Boys—New York (State)--New York--History--20th century--Fiction. | Visions--Fiction. | COVID-19 (Disease)--Fiction. | New York (N.Y.)--History--20th century--Fiction. | LCGFT: Magic realist fiction. | Short stories.
Classification: LCC: PS3618.U7667 P76 2025 | DDC: 813/.6--dc23

Hold fast to dreams

For if dreams die

Life is a broken-winged bird

That cannot fly

Hold fast to dreams

For when dreams go

Life is a barren field

Frozen with snow.

– Langston Hughes

For Pete

Table of Contents

Preface

I originally wrote the following on October 4, 2018.

They Too, Shall Rise

The strapping young man and the lovely young woman approached us as we exited our car near one of several hiking trails we had traversed during our recent vacation in Acadia National Park in Bar Harbor, Maine.

Peggy and I were feeling good about ourselves. After all, we had taken on Jordan Pond, the Jessup Trail and the cliff rocks abutting Sand Beach. Not bad for two old codgers.

The young man had an athletic build as did the young woman, but what struck me was that both were wearing New York Mets garb. In fact, the young man was wearing a Mets jersey adorned with the number 17.

Being a ball buster and a native New Yorker, I felt compelled to rub some salt in the wound. We Noo Yawkers are renowned for that, a trait I actually find admirable.

"Yo, Keith Hernandez. You guys lost or something? Rough year, no?"

Both the young man and the young woman laughed and said, "We'll be back. We just need some bats to augment deGrom, Syndergaard and Wheeler."

We felt at ease with the young couple, who introduced themselves as Don and Pam, man and wife. They were indeed Mets fans, however, Don's southern accent appeared a contradiction.

Almost immediately, we discussed several subjects and Don asked what I did. Upon informing him that I was a writer of sorts and that I had recently written a novel entitled "Prophet's End" which was a tribute to First Responders and paid homage to my idol Pete Hamill and to unworldly beautiful and inspirational Jen Bricker, Don and Pam's interest seemed to increase immensely.

Therefore, since we were literally standing a mere few feet from our car, I opened the trunk and presented them with a copy of "Prophet's End" which I personalized with "To Don and Pam, Follow Your Dreams."

Obviously, this was a pleasant crossing of paths, but I've always been a believer that everything happens for a reason. It was upon returning home to Massachusetts that I learned of a far deeper and resonant fact. There was a note awaiting us, a note which I will share with you. Here it is, verbatim:

Dear Mr. Russell:

It was a pleasure meeting and talking with you and your wife last week in Acadia National Park. As promised, my wife Pam and I each read your book on the flights home this past Saturday and we both enjoyed the story very much.

There were a lot of things in your book that I could relate to very closely (the awesome catch in left field of Game 7 in 1955 because of the stories about the Dodgers my dad used to tell me, the Miracle Mets of '69, and sadly 9/11).

A good friend of mine that I graduated Massapequa High School (NY) with in 1977 lost two cousins with FDNY in the collapse. Please Google "Towers of

Prophet's End

Freedom 9/11 Military Monument" located in John J. Burns Park in Massapequa, N.Y.

My buddy, Frank Haskell built it in remembrance of his cousins and all branches of the Military and victims of 9/11. I visited it last year and it is beautiful. Frank is retired FDNY.

Your book touched me in a way that makes me believe our meeting in Maine was not one of chance, but one of fate and for that I am thankful. Thank you again for the book and may God bless you, sir.

Captain Don R.Stern
Assistant Fire Marshal
City of Tulsa Fire Department
Tulsa, Oklahoma

Acknowledgements

In the summer of 1984, I married a beautiful, partially deaf raven-haired girl named Margaret Jean DiSciullo. Without her, there would be no *Prophet's End* and, in fact, there would most likely be no me. Margaret, or "Peggy" as she is known to her family and friends, has been my savior. Peggy wedded a considerably flawed, emotionally wrecked, most likely suicidal maniac. That would be me. I have often pondered where I would be without her, or perhaps if I would exist at all. Peggy is also a breast cancer survivor.

I've done things in my life I am not proud of. There is no doubt I've hurt several people along the way, but some apologies are discounted, and I do not intend it to appear as if I am worthy of forgiveness. You see, I believe the moral of my volume is that one cannot change the future, and quite truthfully, neither can one alter the present.

The great majority of novels are prefaced with the fictitious disclaimer, "Any resemblance to real persons, living or dead is purely coincidental." So be it, however, in this case, this disclaimer would constitute a blatant lie. I suspect, however, that the publisher, if one actually deems this work suitable for public consumption, will place that very disclaimer in a prominent spot in this novella.

My closest friends in the world, other than my wife of course, hail originally from foreign countries. They are married to each other, a marriage made in heaven. They are Dr. Vladimir Privman and Dr. Violetta Thierbach. Vladimir, born in Uzbekistan, is a New York City endocrinologist. Vladimir, in his youth, was being trained by the Russian KGB. Violetta, a German born in Kazakhstan, has her own dental practice. Incredibly, I've only known them for less than two years. Also, implausibly, I met Vladimir directly owing to our mutual love of music. That is, our love of one particular artist, a young woman named Taimane Gardner, the Hawaiian-born daughter of a Samoan Princess. Taimane, a once in a lifetime artist, is a ukulele virtuoso. Imagine that!

I also wish to acknowledge my doctors, without whom I would not have acquired the strength to even begin this work. You see, I've suffered with Crohn's Disease for well over a decade, an insidious, incurable and anti-immune affliction that is becoming all too prevalent in today's world. Thanks to the wizardry of Dr. Josh Korzenik, a man who has also become a good friend, I am currently in a significant remission. Josh's RN, a young woman named Beth-Ann Norton, has also been a godsend. There are other great physicians as well, too numerous to list, as their names would take up lengthier space than the text of this book. Heartfelt thanks to all.

Pete Hamill is a hero of my tome. Therefore, the fictitious disclaimer would be of no use. It is my belief that all novels are at least, in small part, autobiographical, and *Prophet's End* is no exception. My character "Billy Farrell's" resemblance to yours truly is merely that he grew up (an achievement I've seldom been accused of accomplishing) in the neighborhood I describe as his. That is where the resemblance to Billy begins and ends. Billy is a noble character, I admittedly, am not.

Pete Hamill, as I stated, was an early hero of mine. Mr. Hamill remains an idol of mine, the explanation of which is prevalent throughout this book.

The character "Jennifer Swanson" is beyond a doubt, the heroine of this tale, and once more, the fictitious disclaimer is rendered entirely worthless. That is due to the fact there exists an impossibly beautiful young woman named Jennifer Bricker, and her resemblance to "Jennifer Swanson" is both intentional and the direct result of her inspiration and impact on my life. In truth, Jen Bricker has positively impacted the lives of countless people throughout the world, people of all nationalities, faiths and backgrounds. Jen Bricker, as is "Jen

Swanson" in this book, is the embodiment of beauty and the selfless manifestation of hope and courage.

This tome, then, is all about hope. Without hope, we have nothing

PART I

PROPHET'S END

PROPHET'S END

For all First Responders, Police Officers, and Firefighters everywhere.

Prologue

In 1950s Bronx, New York, Billy Farrell is not an atypical youth. He isn't an atypical ten-year-old, that is, with the exception that Billy Farrell sees things others don't. You see, Billy Farrell can see the future. Not all of the future, mind you; however, glimpses of the future appear to him in dreams. These glimpses are random and they often do not have even a remote significance in Billy's own life.

It was a much simpler time during Billy's youth, a time when seemingly the greatest concern of American youngsters was how to avoid the dreaded Russians by squeezing oneself under a wooden school desk during practiced bomb shelter air raids. Paranoia over the threat of communism was rampant, and even more importantly, would the Brooklyn Dodgers ever defeat the New York Yankees in the World Series? Billy was a huge Dodgers fan and in the iconic season of 1955, that idea dominated his thoughts, other than his constant daydreaming regarding his little brunette classmate, Audrey Simmons. Would she ever notice him?

Billy Farrell, the son of Irish immigrants from Belfast, Northern Ireland, was a good student, not a great one, but his teachers loved him because he was considerate, thoughtful, and he tried hard to please. And he sure loved the Brooklyn Dodgers!

Billy was also an avid reader. It was that inclination that provided him with his first hero, a young aspiring columnist with the *New York Post*, a man who would go on to be recognized as one of the greatest journalists and authors in American history, Pete Hamill, himself the son of Irish immigrants from Belfast. Incredibly,

Pete Hamill would become a close friend of Billy and under extraordinary circumstances.

Chapter One

Growing up here, you learned one bitter lesson: whenever something was destroyed for "the crime of being old, what replaced it was infinitely worse. – Pete Hamill

Billy Farrell was six years old when he first saw the girl in a dream. It was 1951, and Billy was in the first grade in elementary school at P.S. 61 in the South Bronx in New York City. She was approximately, Billy thought, his own age. She appeared as a visage one early morning as he was in that period between slumber and awakening. Her face was round and pretty, her eyes sparkled, and she seemed to smile. Billy seemed confused, he had never thought much about girls, but this one was different, he thought.

As for real girls, Billy's classmate in the first and second grade at P.S. 61 at 1550 Crotona Park East, was a pretty, slender girl named Audrey Simmons. Billy liked the way she laughed and the fact that she seemed very smart; however, Billy was shy, awkward, and a bit clumsy and Audrey paid him little or no attention. As luck would have it, several years later, Billy would attend Morris High School and would reunite with his classmate Audrey while both were freshmen in high school. Billy would sit behind Audrey in some of their classes and stare languidly at the back of her head. Although Billy had grown out of his awkwardness, he still remained quite shy with girls. However, his hormones were just beginning to kick in.

As Billy's adolescence progressed, the face of the young girl in his dreams would appear to him more frequently and as he grew, so did the visage. She appeared to age commensurately with Billy. By the time he was ten, Billy would often daydream about the girl he had never met and wondered why she consumed his dreams. By the time

Billy was sixteen years old, he developed his initial crush on a girl who, he reasoned, did not even exist. Billy never spoke to anyone about his recurring dream for fear of being ridiculed.

The New York of Billy's childhood is no longer in existence. The South Bronx of his youth had large maple trees lining his neighborhood on Crotona Park East. Around the corner on Wilkins Avenue, there was a candy store, an ice cream parlor with wrought iron chairs with heart shaped backs and where a soda jerk would offer delicious egg creams, hot fudge and strawberry sundaes, root beer floats and malted milks and these delectable delights would be served in tall glasses. There was no graffiti on the walls.

In the Crotona Park of yesteryear, Billy would play with many of his young friends. There was Tony the Wop, Kevin the Mick, Lenny the Kike, and many others with nicknames which were not meant to demean, but to identify. It was an age before political correctness removed the alleged stigma of belonging to an ethnic group, as if it were derogatory. Everyone had each other's backs, so to speak, and no outsider was permitted to address Billy and his friends in such a manner. Lenny was a Kike, but he was "their kike," and so on. The names were administered, and each youngster considered it a badge of honor. It was a privilege to be accepted.

Billy and his younger brother, Evan, lived with their parents, Brian and Kathleen, in a tenement building at 1428 Crotona Park East in a third-floor apartment which overlooked Crotona Park. The huge maple trees which lined the street would provide shade for the elderly Jewish and Italian women who would congregate on the park benches facing the tenements. These women knew everyone and everything and gossiped freely about everyone in the area. They served as the eyes and ears of the community.

Billy's parents, Brian and Kathleen, were both immigrants from Belfast in Northern Ireland. Brian worked as a longshoreman and Kathleen a housewife. In the early 1950s, American paranoia over "The Cold War" even reached elementary school. Our government's preoccupation and fear of dreaded "communism" permeated our lives despite the fact that the great majority of the American public could not even define the word "communism." The irrational fears resulted in a truly dark era of the United States, "The McCarthy Witch Hunt," a misguided investigation of those in politics and the entertainment industry, one headed by a previously obscure Senator named Joe McCarthy. His "House Committee on Un-American Activities" resulted in many innocent people losing their livelihoods and in some cases, their lives. Successful Hollywood careers were tarnished and ruined forever.

It was at the height of "The Cold War" that the absurd level of paranoia even managed to reach elementary schools, including Billy's P.S. 61 in the Bronx. Fearing a Russian atomic bomb attack, "Air Raid Drills" were initiated in public schools. Warning sirens sounded and students were instructed to dip beneath their wooden desks in a "duck and cover" maneuver. Billy and his classmates would crouch underneath their desks, facing away from the windows to protect against flying debris and glass. Then in 1953 Russia exploded its first hydrogen bomb. The Russians are coming! The Russians are coming! The illogical foolishness even reached major league baseball where the storied franchise the Cincinnati Reds changed their name to the Cincinnati Redlegs, not to be confused with the Chinese communists or the Russian "Reds."

Chapter Two

It was the year 1955 when Billy finally began to have dreams other than ones that revolved around the pretty girl with the dark hair and lovely round face. Billy loved baseball, and in particular, his beloved Brooklyn Dodgers. Billy's parents, Brian and Kathleen, were, of course, immigrants from Belfast in Northern Ireland, and although neither was interested in baseball, they encouraged their sons, Billy, ten, and his younger brother, Evan, eight, to pursue "American interests."

Billy watched the Dodgers on the family's twelve-inch black-and-white television in their third-floor Crotona Park East apartment. Billy was also permitted to listen to the Dodger games on his transistor radio as long as he had finished his homework. This was never a problem as Billy was an excellent student and one becoming increasingly interested in the art of writing.

The year 1955 was an iconic one for Billy's beloved Brooklyn Dodgers as they finally provided optimism to their faithful that they were capable of finally defeating their dreaded rivals, the New York Yankees, who seemed like perennial world champions. The Dodgers, although formidable in prior years, would seemingly always crumble when going head to head against the inhabitants of Yankee Stadium.

The classic World Series of 1955 came down to a winner take all seventh game and when Brian arrived home and surprised Billy with four tickets to the game at the historic Bronx venue. Billy was as thrilled as he had ever been during his brief lifetime. Kathleen, Billy's mom, reminded her husband that the game was during a school day. However, Brian responded, "The lad is a fine student. I'm certain his teachers will understand." In fact, for the penultimate game six, the teachers had suspended class so that their students could hear the game on the radio.

Billy was so excited later that evening, that he could hardly sleep. It was approximately 1:00 A.M. when he finally drifted off, but for the initial time since he commenced dreaming, his dream was not of the pretty brunette with the round face, but of the historic seventh game of the World Series he was about to witness in person.

The vision in the dream was not crystal clear except for an amazing catch performed by a relatively obscure outfielder named Sandy Amoros. The vague details included Johnny Podres, the Dodgers young left-handed pitcher winning the game 2-0. Gil Hodges, Billy's favorite player on the Dodgers, would drive in both runs. However, the lucent vision which shocked Billy was that of an unlikely hero, a young Cuban outfielder named Edmundo Isasi "Sandy" Amoros. In Billy's vivid portion of the dream, Amoros, playing left field in the bottom of the sixth inning, would race to the left field corner, just a mere few feet from the foul pole and make a remarkable one handed catch, wheel and fire a strike to Dodger shortstop "Pee Wee" Reese, who in turn would throw a strike to Dodger first baseman Gil Hodges to complete a miraculous game saving double play. The image was indelible.

Billy awoke on that fateful day of October 4, 1955 with a sense of excitement and joy. Billy was both fascinated and confused in regard to his dream, which was both surrealistic and unimaginable. After all, he had never experienced a dream even remotely similar. Invariably, Billy's dreams revolved around the visage of the pretty little brunette girl with the round face, the girl who didn't even exist, he thought. Why would he suddenly experience a dream about the baseball game he was about to attend? Billy also reasoned that the final score in the dream, 2-0 in favor of the Dodgers, was extremely unlikely, since both the Yankees and Dodgers were renowned for their formidable offenses.

Billy rationalized he dreamed that Gil Hodges would drive in both runs because of the fact that Hodges was Billy's favorite player. He laughed when he thought of the absurdity of Amoros making an exceptional game saving catch. It wasn't as if Sandy Amoros wasn't a decent fielder, however, he was a rather obscure reserve player and in the projected lineups printed by the New York major dailies, Amoros wasn't even slated to start the game.

At 11:00 A.M., Brian and Kathleen gathered Billy and Evan and walked over to the IRT Subway station in order to head towards Yankee Stadium. Very few of the folks in that area had cars in those days. Upon switching to the Woodlawn Road train #4 at 149th Street, Billy's excitement grew as he anticipated seeing his heroes in their quest for the elusive World Series championship. The Brooklyn Dodgers had appeared in six prior World Series, but had never emerged victoriously. Billy fervently wished that his dream portended something wonderful was about to occur. Billy, of course, did not speak of his vision, not to his parents and not to his younger brother, Evan, who was more enthusiastic about the prospect of devouring ice cream and hot dogs than the game itself.

As the train entered the 161st Street and River Avenue subway stop, Billy's excitement reached fever pitch. The family walked purposefully to the gates, where Brian handed the ticket taker the four passes, and the Farrells were allowed passage into Yankee Stadium. Their seats were in grandstand Section One upstairs, behind home plate. After our National Anthem was played with the Yankees standing at their respective positions, Tommy Byrne, the veteran Yankees pitcher began his warm-ups. Billy suddenly recalled his dream of the night before. He remembered the vague part of the dream, the one where he saw his hero Gil Hodges knock in both runs in a complete game shutout by southpaw Johnny Podres. So, in the fourth inning when Hodges singled to drive in Roy Campanella giving the Dodgers a 1-0 lead, he cheered and smiled at the "coincidence."

Meanwhile, Johnny Podres was indeed pitching shutout ball, just as he had done in the dream. When Gil Hodges drove "Pee Wee" Reese home with a sacrifice fly in the top of the sixth inning, Billy cheered and also recalled the details of his dream. Billy thought to himself as Reese crossed home plate with the second run, that the probability of Amoros making a game saving catch was nil. After all, Amoros was not even in the game! However, when Dodger outfielder George "Shotgun" Shuba entered the game as a pinch-hitter for second baseman Don Zimmer shortly after Hodges's sacrifice fly, Billy's wheels began turning.

The move by Dodger manager, Walter Alston, would necessitate changes on defense. Therefore, when the Dodgers took the field to begin the bottom half of the sixth inning, Dodger left fielder Jim Gilliam switched to second base and Sandy Amoros entered the game as a defensive replacement in left field!

Billy immediately became animated, although he would still not inform his parents of his potentially being realized dream. Instead, he suddenly grabbed his father, Brian, by the hand and exclaimed, "C'mon, Dad!" Billy's dad reacted with some confusion, thinking that perhaps his son wanted to go to the restroom or the concessions stand, but what Billy wanted to do was to walk towards the left field grandstand in order to see Amoros's impending historical catch!

As Billy and his father stood upstairs near the left field foul pole, Brian asked his son, "What's this all about, lad?"

Billy replied, "You'll see, Dad."

When both Yankee stalwarts, Billy Martin and Gil McDougald, reached base to begin the inning, it appeared as if Dodger hurler Johnny Podres was on the ropes. There were runners on first and second and no one out. The next hitter was Yankee great "Yogi" Berra, who stood menacingly at the plate representing the lead run. When Berra sliced a long drive into the left field corner near the foul pole, the sold out crowd at Yankee Stadium held its collective breath. Sandy Amoros, the diminutive fleet footed Cuban, just inserted into the game for defensive purposes, seemingly came out of nowhere. Extending his right gloved hand while on the full gallop, he made a miraculous catch, spun and threw a strike to shortstop "Pee Wee" Reese, who in turn, fired a strike to Dodger first baseman Gil Hodges, who stretched for the throw which doubled Yankee base runner Gil McDougald off of first base. Double play! Exactly the sequence in Billy's dream!

The Dodgers went on and indeed, won the game 2-0 as Billy had also seen, but with less clarity. Upon returning to their seats behind home plate, Brian remarked to his wife, Kathleen.

"The lad apparently must have had a premonition. He took me to left field and we got to see the extraordinary catch. Pure luck!"

Billy was not about to tell his dad that the historic play was much more than pure luck.

Chapter Three

In 1957, two years after the unusual, but foretelling "Sandy Amoros Dream," Billy experienced another even more bizarre vision that was seemingly innocuous, but one that rendered the youngster confused and bewildered. As he lay in bed in the early morning hours, Billy grew restless. Suddenly, it was as if he was on a roller coaster and had entered some sort of wormhole. Intense and fleeting visions were coming at him at a frenetic pace. It was as if the boy had become entangled in some sort of time travel.

The youth began twitching and despite being asleep, his eyes opened wide and began rolling in his head. What began as a brief absurd image quickly evolved into some sort of surreal newsreel gone mad. First, he saw a rotund, bald man in a suit, seated at a table at which he was banging his shoe on at a place called the UN. The man seemed perturbed and he looked like someone's grandfather.

Following were a compendium of visions resembling highway signs being passed by a speeding vehicle, with the images arriving faster than the boy could manage to absorb them. He saw children and young adults all gyrating with hoops twirling around their hips and waists. He had a vision of four shaggy-haired mop-topped young men singing and performing on stage as young teenage girls went berserk and fainted.

Billy watched in a cacophony of silent and yet deafening sound, sort of a mute eloquence of absurdity. He saw a handsome, brown-skinned, superbly conditioned prize fighter standing over his fallen opponent, taunting him and mouthing the words, "Get up!"

The dizzying, delirious concoction of images seemed like ancient hieroglyphics or Sanskrit to the young boy. At once, he saw thousands of black people and white people, arm in arm, as they marched together with Washington's Capitol Building in the background. The people all appeared grim, but determined.

Several additional scenes flew by at an almost giddy pace. The decades were advancing at warp speed. At once, a new millennium had begun. Suddenly, there was an implosion and everything went black. The alarm clock had gone off.

As Billy grew a bit older, his recurrent dream, the one in which he merely saw the visage of the pretty brunette girl, increased in quantity. In the dreams, she never spoke. He just saw her attractive face, a face that appeared to continue to grow in age commensurately with his age. By 1961, Billy was sixteen years old and no longer as awkward or clumsy. However, Billy, still a bright student, was shy with the opposite sex; although a handsome youth, girls his age found him attractive. Billy's hormones were just about to kick in as he entered his freshman year at Morris High School in the South Bronx.

Morris High, at 166th Street and Boston Road, was noted for its impressive tower and was a terrific place for Billy to continue his formal education. Its alumni included "The King of Comedy" Milton Berle, famous dancer Arthur Murray, and Herman Joseph Muller, a Nobel Prize Winner in Medicine in the year 1946. Billy was at this point of his young life, a great student and a voracious reader. Therefore, he decided to attempt his hand at a career in journalism and joined the school newspaper, *The Tower*, which was both encouraged and recommended by his teachers.

Billy read newspapers ravenously, and in the New York of 1961, there were a multitude of major dailies, and being from a liberal household as both his mom, Kathleen and dad, Brian, being sensitive to injustice, something they were both subjected to in their youth in Northern Ireland, Billy's favorite newspaper was the renowned left-leaning *New York Post*.

The Editor-in-Chief at the *Post* was a crusty middle-aged, hard-drinking, chain-smoking tousled haired man named James Wechsler, who was a renowned fighter for civil rights, labor, and the underdog in general. Billy's dad would read the *Post* religiously and discuss world events with his eager son. In particular, young Billy had developed an affinity for a young writer at the *Post*, a twenty-six-year-old aspiring journalist named Pete Hamill. Hamill at the time toiled as a beat writer who covered murders and fires, but penned an occasional column. Billy loved the manner in which Hamill strung words together as did Billy's dad, Brian. Brian referred to the young journalist as a "wordsmith." Hamill, Billy felt, wrote about New York City and its inhabitants with a grace, style, and flair which seemed beyond imagination. Billy loved Hamill's passion and his utter disdain for injustice, blowhards and phonies. Upon seeing his father bring home the evening edition of the *Post* each night, Billy would anxiously flip through the pages in hope of finding an event or occurrence that Hamill covered. Upon finding something written by Pete Hamill, Billy would never be disappointed.

As a freshman in high school, Billy was pleased upon seeing that Audrey Simmons, his elementary school classmate, was once more in several of his classes. He had not seen her for several years and now she appeared even more attractive to him, since he was quickly growing into manhood and Audrey into womanhood. This time, however, Audrey, who never paid much attention to the younger, awkward Billy Farrell, was attracted to the now handsome and intelligent young man. Billy, although still quite shy, was surprised when Audrey caught him peering at her and smiled at him. It gave him a funny feeling he was not familiar with, a good feeling.

Meanwhile, as the school year progressed, Billy's dreams of the mysterious girl with the round face were becoming more frequent. Her visage now haunted his waking hours as well, as he frequently daydreamed about her, wondering who she was and why she possessed his thoughts, and with his hormones kicking in, he found her alluring. As alluring, that is, as a young lady can be to a teenager lacking in maturity.

Something else began to occur during Billy's sleeping hours; for the first time since 1955 when he dreamed in advance of the Brooklyn Dodgers World Series victory, he began to experience visions of the future, other than the weird "newsreel dream" he briefly endured. It began oddly enough with another baseball incident, this despite the fact that Billy's interest in baseball had waned. His beloved Dodgers had departed for Los Angeles in 1958, and that plus the fact that he now enjoyed other arts and endeavors lessened his love for the game of baseball. Therefore, he thought it strange when he experienced a vivid dream that involved a team and a player he wasn't even following.

On the evening of Monday May 8, 1961, Billy, now sixteen years of age, completed his homework, made sure to read the *New York Times* and as was his wont, the *New York Post*, and went to bed. He was about to have that unforeseen dream. As he lay in the darkness, Billy began to see images of a baseball game, a game at a place called Metropolitan Stadium in Minneapolis. Distinctly, he envisioned this tall strapping left handed hitter step up to the plate and he saw the name "Jim Gentile" listed in block letters below his image. Gentile was wearing a Baltimore Orioles uniform. Billy noticed that the bases were loaded and it was the top of the first inning.

Although not even remotely interested in the game, he watched as a Minnesota Twin pitcher delivered a pitch which Gentile immediately blasted over the fence for a grand slam home run, a rare feat by itself. As the dream continued, he once more saw Jim Gentile step to the plate with the bases loaded. Was this a dream replay? Billy soon noticed that it was not and that the game had entered the second inning. Once more, Jim Gentile swung the bat and hit still another grand slam home run! Back to back grand slam home runs on successive pitches, as well. When Billy awoke that morning, his odd dream remained vivid in his mind.

Billy entered the kitchen for breakfast and found the morning edition of the *New York Daily News* where his father had left it on the kitchen table. He turned to the sports section and read that evening's pitching probable pitchers. He immediately saw that the Baltimore Orioles were indeed, playing the Minnesota Twins at Metropolitan Stadium in Baltimore later that evening. He suddenly thought back to his prophetic dream of six years earlier, when Sandy Amoros had made his now memorable catch in game seven of the iconic World Series in 1955.

Still hesitant to inform anyone of his questionable gift, if that's indeed, what it was, Billy pondered if he should inform someone regarding the possibility that he had somehow unwittingly and unknowingly acquired some form of clairvoyance. Therefore, he went to school that day, but, following class, he told his mom that he'd be late that afternoon. Billy, now sixteen years of age and trustworthy and mature, took the IRT Subway down to Manhattan. He hoped to meet his idol, the columnist and writer for the *New York Post*, Pete Hamill.

As Billy rode the subway to his destination, he had absolutely no idea what he was going to say to Pete Hamill if he actually met him; however, he was compelled to at least try.

Chapter Four

As Billy emerged from the subway in the heart of Manhattan, he was awe struck by the size of the buildings and the thousands of people scurrying in every conceivable direction, all seemingly with a sense of purpose. It wasn't as if the boy was experiencing his initial trip to the Big Apple, since his parents had taken him to Radio City Music Hall, Carnegie Hall, and Madison Square Garden, however, this was indeed, his first excursion alone. The youngster, although slightly overwhelmed by the vast city, suddenly recalled his own goal as he approached the offices of the *New York Post*, the headquarters of his idol, journalist Pete Hamill.

Billy entered the offices of the *New York Post* and the somewhat shy sixteen year-old asked a pleasant and attractive young receptionist if Mr. Hamill was in. The young lady paused, stared at the polite youngster and asked quizzically, "Do you have an appointment with Mr. Hamill?"

"No ma'am, but I'd only take a few moments."

The young woman, responded, "Well, I think you may be in luck. This is one of the occasions that Pete is in the office. Just go down this hallway and turn left. I believe you'll find him in the second room on the right."

"Thank you, ma'am."

"Aren't you polite?!" she exclaimed and smiled at the attractive youngster.

Pete Hamill sat at a chair overlooking the street below and he and the Editor-in-Chief, James Wechsler, were deep in conversation.

Wechsler had a cigarette in his hand and his ashtray was overflowing with cigarette butts. Wechsler sported shirt sleeves and a bow-tie and appeared slightly disheveled. Wechsler seemed a bit perturbed.

"Dorothy doesn't want me speaking to Doyle that way. How else am I going to get his ass to provide the information we need? Screw her!"

Dorothy Schiff was the Publisher of the *N.Y. Post*.

Pete Hamill responded, "Frank Doyle is the Press Secretary for the entire New York City Police Department. Hell, wasn't he a reporter for the *N.Y. Daily Mirror*?"

"Yeah, Pete, but sometimes I think he forgot about us peons. I'll just have to exercise more tact."

Suddenly, both James Wechsler and Pete Hamill became aware of the youngster standing in their doorway with a look of astonishment and awe on his face. Pete Hamill was the first to speak.

"Can I help you, young man?" Billy gulped before replying.

"You're Pete Hamill! I mean Mr. Hamill."

"The last time I checked, I was. And with whom do I have the pleasure of speaking?"

"I'm Billy. I'm a student at Morris High School in the Bronx and I write for our school newspaper and I think you're great!"

"How old are you, Billy?"

"I'm sixteen."

James Wechsler responded to the telephone ringing. "It's Dorothy! I'll see you later."

With that, Wechsler arose from his seat and as he left the room, he turned to Billy.

"Nice meeting you, young man. When you graduate, perhaps we can use a cub reporter."

Pete Hamill then spoke.

"Thanks for the compliment, Billy. You made my day."

"I love the way you write about the city, Mr. Hamill."

"It's Pete, not 'Mr.,' Billy."

Pete Hamill paused before continuing.

"So, what brings you here, Billy?"

"I have these dreams, really weird dreams. I see things in the future."

"Can you give me an example, Billy?"

"When I was ten, in 1955, I dreamed the Dodgers would win the World Series. I dreamed of Sandy Amoros's catch the night before it happened."

Pete Hamill peered at young Billy and appeared skeptical although Billy did not pick up on his incredulity. Pete liked Billy, however, now realized that he was no doubt dealing with someone either delusional or putting him on.

"Oh? That was a helluva catch! Without Sandy's play, the Dodgers most likely would have lost that game and it would still be 'wait until next year'."

Pete laughed and hesitated before continuing.

"Can you tell me what the lottery numbers will be tonight, Billy?"

"My dreams are random, I'm afraid, sir. I keep dreaming about a pretty girl with dark hair and a round face, but I don't think she even exists."

Pete Hamill laughed once more before responding. "Ha! I've had a few dreams about girls like that, too!"

Billy appeared briefly confused, but composed himself to speak.

"It's not like that, Mr., I mean Pete, all I see is this girl's face. I've never met her."

Pete leaned back in his chair before replying. "Have you had any other dreams recently, Billy?"

"Yes, sir, Pete, I had a vivid dream last night. I saw a guy hit two grand slam home runs in back to back at bats in the first and second inning."

Pete smiled and replied. He was humoring the boy.

"Was it Mickey Mantle?"

"No, actually it was Jim Gentile."

"Jim Gentile of the Baltimore Orioles?"

"Yes, Jim Gentile of the Orioles. And he's going to hit them tonight."

Pete paused and picked the morning paper off of his desk. He flipped to the sports section and read that Baltimore was in Minnesota to play the Twins.

"Back to back home runs in successive innings, huh, Billy? That would be quite a feat."

Billy, of course, did not realize that Pete Hamill was toying with him. "Yes, Pete, and on successive pitches."

"That's even more impressive, son."

At that point, James Wechsler returned and stood in the doorway.

"Pete, Dorothy wants us both in her office. She's got Doyle on the horn and he's livid."

Pete arose from his seat and grasped Billy's hand and spoke. "Sorry, but I have to go. Nice meeting you!"

Billy thanked his hero and walked out of the office, but not before getting Pete to sign an edition of that evening's *New York Post*.

Chapter Five

On the morning of Wednesday, May 10, 1961, Billy awoke and sleepily sauntered to the kitchen where Brian, his dad, was having breakfast and reading the morning edition of the *Daily News*. Billy was actually half-hoping that his dream did not bear fruition, these visions were beginning to frighten him, all that is, except the recurrent vision of the pretty brunette girl with the round face.

"Can I see the sports section, Dad?"

"Of course, you can, lad. Didja see what that Baltimore hitter accomplished last night in Minnesota, son?"

"Was it Jim Gentile, Dad?"

"How didja know, lad? You must've been listening to your transistor radio while in bed last evening. Don't worry, I won't tell your mom."

Billy glanced briefly at the headline in the sports section which read,

Gentile Blasts Two Grand Slam Homers in Historic Feat

Billy did not even have to read the article to know they came in the initial two innings of the game. As he prepared for his school day, Billy paused while brushing his teeth and stared into the mirror. He wondered exactly who the sixteen-year-old peering back at him really was. Why me? Why was I chosen to receive these foretelling dreams? What force allowed him to foresee these events? Will these visions persist or was the Amoros catch and Jim Gentile's historic feat just periodic glimpses into the future?

Billy also pondered whether or not he should tell anyone of his gift, if that's what it was. Would they question his sanity? Would they

suggest psychiatric observation? And what about the pretty little brunette girl, as her visage was becoming even more prevalent during the
hours he slept. Billy was actually becoming slightly aroused by her
"presence," although all he saw was her face. Was I losing my mind?
Am I possessed by some demon?

At school that day, Billy's concentration waned. He was extremely hesitant about the prospect of informing anyone about his
predicament, if it indeed, was actually a dilemma. Then suddenly he
recalled meeting his idol, Pete Hamill, the previous afternoon.

Chapter Six

Pete Hamill, bleary eyed, rushed into the offices of the *New York Post*. James Wechsler was seated at his desk, smoking a cigarette and typing furiously. He seemed possessed and was slightly startled when Hamill interrupted him breathlessly.

"Billy, the boy who was here yesterday, do you recall his name?"

"Yeah, you just said it, it's Billy."

Hamill laughed at Wechsler's intentional wiseass response before continuing.

"I know that, Jimmy. I mean did he offer his last name?"

"Not that I recall. I seem to remember he said he wrote for his high school paper in the Bronx. Was it Roosevelt High, Monroe High, or Samuel Gompers?"

Wechsler took a deep drag on his cigarette and responded.

"Perhaps Morris High?"

Pete snapped his fingers.

"Yeah, I think that's it! I've got to find him!"

"What's this all about, Pete?"

"I not sure, Jimmy. This kid may have some real special gifts. He sees things"

James Wechsler chuckled.

"Hell, I see things, too. I just saw something this morning that I wish to God that I could unsee!

"What was so ghastly, Jimmy?"

"I just saw Erma Bombeck wearing shorts!" (Erma Bombeck was a heavyset humorist and syndicated columnist.) Hamill laughed up-roariously before replying. "Jesus, I just ate! That is some disturbing imagery."

"Hey, Pete, if the kid is truly gifted, tell him he can intern here this summer."

"Sure, Jimmy."

Pete Hamill was not certain that he should inform his boss and friend of Billy's gifts. He had a hunch that the youngster may endanger himself. Hamill made a mental note to call Morris High School in order to learn which students wrote for the school paper. He knew that correctly forecasting Jim Gentile's historic feat was not some sort of accidental chance. Something truly bizarre was afoot.

Chapter Seven

Upon calling Morris High School, Pete was informed that there were three youngsters named William contributing to the school's newspaper, *The Tower*. Pete planned to visit Morris High that Friday in order to seek out the seemingly clairvoyant Billy. He wouldn't have to.

Later that afternoon, Pete Hamill sat alone in his office. He had just returned from a meeting with Mayor Wagner at Gracie Mansion, the official residence of the Mayor of New York, Robert F. Wagner, when he looked up from his desk and saw Billy, once more standing outside the doorway of his office.

Before Pete could even greet his unexpected visitor, the boy spoke.

"I'm scared, Pete. I'm really scared."

Pete Hamill arose from his chair, walked over to Billy and put his arm around him. He closed the door to his office.

"I can understand, son. Have you shared this gift with anyone other than me, Billy?"

"No sir, I haven't. You're the only person I've told about it."

"Not even your parents?"

"No sir, not even them. I love them, but I don't want them thinking I'm crazy."

"You mentioned knowing about the Amoros catch? You never told anyone about that?"

"No sir, I was only ten."

Billy paused briefly before continuing.

"I'm really scared, Pete. Why is this happening to me? Why me? Why was I chosen and by whom was I chosen?"

Pete stared out of the window onto the streets of Gotham, deep in thought.

"Billy, you've got my word. I'll never tell anyone. If you have any other dreams or visions, please know that you can trust me. I'm not sure that it would be wise to allow anyone to know that on occasion you have these visions that all seem to be realized."

Pete reached for a pen on his desk and began scribbling a note. "Billy, this is my home telephone. Not too many folks know it. Call me at any time. I mean it."

"You don't know how much I appreciate that, Pete."

"Tell me, Billy, you mentioned this recurring dream or vision about a young girl. What's your gut feeling? Do you think she really exists? I mean, Sandy Amoros and Jim Gentile certainly exist!"

"Gee, I don't know, sir. All I do know is that she's real pretty and that she makes me feel funny, if you know what I mean. But I can only see her face."

"Billy, does she ever speak in your dreams?"

"No sir, she's silent and there's one more thing. I began seeing her when I was six, but she's grown as I have. She seems to get older as I do. She looks about sixteen, my age."

Pete walked over to the window, seemingly deep in thought.

"I've got an idea, Billy. Can you describe her? You know, can you describe her facial features and complexion? You're a writer, I suspect that you can."

"I can give it a try, Pete. Let's see, she's got dark hair."

Pete interrupted Billy. "No, don't describe her to me. I'm going to bring in a sketch artist from the New York Police Department. He's a good friend of mine. You won't have to tell him why he's drawing her."

"Sure, Pete, I can do that. He works for the Police Department? I've often thought that one day I can become a police officer or a writer, Mr. Hamill."

Pete Hamill laughed before responding.

"I knew I liked you, Billy! Wow, two thankless jobs, not one! By the way, Billy, what's your full name?"

"It's William Fitzgerald Farrell, sir. My parents are from Belfast in Northern Ireland."

"Are you kidding me, Billy? My parents are also from Belfast!"

"I'm aware of that, Pete. You wrote about them in one of your columns."

"Wow, you really do read my work!"

"When should I come in to meet the sketch artist, Pete?"

"I'm having lunch with him tomorrow. Can you get here after school?"

"I sure can, I'm looking forward to solving this mystery."

"You're not the only one, that is, Billy."

Chapter Eight

Ed Barrow, the slender middle-aged African American sketch art-ist for the NYPD, smiled at Billy as he sat in Pete Hamill's office at the *New York Post*. He had just completed the drawing of the young round faced beauty of Billy's dreams. Ed Barrow spoke.

"I wish more of the people I dealt with were as descriptive as you are, Billy. I believe you've got a great future in communications. So, how did we do?"

"You've really captured exactly the way she looks, Mr. Barrow. Wow, you can really draw!"

"Who is she, Billy? Is she missing?"

"I'm not exactly sure who she is, sir. I just saw her a few times."

Billy hesitated before continuing.

"I'm not even sure if she exists."

Ed Barrow laughed before responding.

"Well, I hope you find out she's real, Billy. She's really pretty, whoever she is!"

Pete Hamill arose from his chair and shook Ed Barrow's hand before replying.

"Thanks again, Ed. Will I see you at ringside for the Denny Moyer fight at the Garden this Friday?"

"If I can escape from the wife, I'll be there, Pete. Say, who is this girl I just drew, anyhow?"

Pete Hamill winked at Barrow and answered, "Damned if I know!"

Chapter Nine

In the year 1963, as the burgeoning career of twenty-eight-year-old Pete Hamill ascended to new heights, eighteen-year-old Billy's horizons also expanded as he was rapidly growing out of his awkwardness and the intelligent, handsome youth was quickly evolving into a young man. However, during the year, Pete Hamill was in the midst of a major career change, one that would relocate him to Europe to begin anew as a contributing editor to *The Saturday Evening Post*.

Despite the fact that Billy was flourishing as a young man, he continued to have dreams and visions of the beautiful dark-haired girl with the round face, and as he had experienced before, she continued to seem to grow commensurately in age with him. However, she still remained silent in the dreams and only appeared as a visage. Hamill would call from Europe on occasion, but the differences in time zones and their lives precluded a closer relationship.

Billy, now a senior at Morris High, had begun to date the girl he had earlier had a crush on, Audrey Simmons, his classmate, but then Billy had a life-altering dream. Audrey was enamored with Billy and he, in turn, found her extremely attractive; however, his dream suddenly and entirely forever revised his relationship with Audrey.

One evening in early spring, only weeks before he was to take Audrey to the senior prom, Billy had a vivid dream about the beautiful girl with the round face. In the vision, Billy saw himself in a church, surrounded by friends and family seated in pews. He stood in front of the altar and turned to see a young woman seated, not standing, next to him. She wore a beautiful white wedding dress and a veil. In the dream, he lifted the veil and there sat the beautiful girl with the dark hair, the girl he had constantly dreamed about! He was about to marry her!

Prophet's End

Billy's dreams to that point invariably bore fruition without exception. Therefore, he knew in his heart and mind that he would someday marry this girl despite the fact that he had no idea who she was. He also knew that not only was this the girl of his dreams, but that she was **LITERALLY** that.

In early June of 1961, Billy had what he thought an absurd vision. He dreamed that a baseball player named Roger Maris would hit a historic home run on October 1st against a pitcher he had never heard of, Tracy Stallard. If that wasn't ridiculous enough, in the dream, the ball would be caught by a truck driver from Brooklyn named Sal Durante. He had informed Pete Hamill of this vision, and although they both shared a great laugh, both Hamill and Billy were certain the event would take place, and when it did, all Hamill could do was to shake his head and laugh uproariously and lament the fact that Las Vegas provided no odds for predicting that sort of outcome.

Meanwhile, before the dream of his impending wedding, Audrey Simmons, Billy's senior prom date and girlfriend, frequently spoke to Billy about someday being wed to him. After all, she considered them high school sweethearts and she was smitten with him.

Billy, of course, had never confided any of his dreams to anyone other than Pete Hamill, his mentor and friend. Audrey, a good friend, and Brian and Kathleen, Billy's mom and dad, were never made privy to Billy's incredible visions. Therefore, one day in early May, Audrey, playfully and somewhat wistfully brought up the subject of perhaps marrying Billy in the future. Billy's immediate reaction was one that he would almost immediately regret.

"Listen, Audrey, you know that I think the world of you. You're pretty, you're smart, you make me laugh all the time, and you're incredibly nice."

Audrey peered at Billy quizzically before responding.

"Well, those are all good things, but?"

There was a significant pregnant pause.

Billy took a deep breath before replying.

"But I can never marry you, Audrey."

Audrey appeared almost bemused, as if Billy was prefacing a punch line for some sort of joke.

"And why not?"

Audrey's face was a combination of intrigue, confusion and expectation.

"Because I already know who I'm going to marry well, sort of."

Audrey appeared hurt and fairly bewildered and replied softly. "What?"

Billy answered, but with a considerable amount of trepidation. He was about to tell the first person other than Pete Hamill of a frequent dream he experienced.

"I know who I'm going to marry, Audrey. I've dreamed about her many times."

Tears welled in Audrey's eyes.

"Who is she? Do I know her?"

By this time, Billy realized that he should have never initiated the conversation, but had no alternative but to continue it.

"I've never met her, Audrey. I don't even know her name."

Audrey sobbed briefly, but composed herself to respond.

"Is this some sort of sick joke? It's not funny, Billy."

"I'm sorry, Audrey. I'm just telling you the truth. I'm sorry if I hurt you."

Audrey responded with a combination of anger, confusion and hurt. "Hurt me?! Hurt me?! You're going to marry some imaginary girl?! Are you sick, Billy?"

Billy Farrell hung his head. For the initial time since he began having these visions, he realized how ridiculously absurd they appeared to a sentient being.

Audrey ran out of the room crying. She would not attend the senior prom with Billy. Billy, in fact, would not attend the prom. When Audrey's mother asked why Billy was not taking her daughter to the prom, Audrey responded, "He's with his imaginary girlfriend."

Chapter Ten

In the early morning hours of Friday, November 22, 1963, Billy awoke from his slumber. He had gone to bed the night before suffering from a severe head cold. He had overslept. It was approximately 8:00 A.M. and as he arose from bed, Billy's shirt was soaked with sweat. Billy was practically hyperventilating as he cried out, "Oh, my God!"

Billy had experienced a horrific dream, but all that he could recall was seeing a motorcade traveling through downtown Dallas, Texas. His dear friend Pete Hamill was now in Europe, most likely in Paris or London, and the local time there was early afternoon. Billy was in complete panic mode. This was a time way before the advent of cell phones.

Billy had, of course, never notified anyone other than Hamill of his dreams, visions that had all come true. How in hell could he possibly reach anyone in order to prevent this atrocious act from taking place? Would they come and place him in a strait jacket? Would they think him complicit because of his prior knowledge?

Billy searched for the telephone number Pete had given him before he relocated to Europe. Upon finding it, Billy dialed it feverishly, but got Hamill's answering machine. The overwrought Billy left a brief fearful message.

"Pete, it's Billy. Please dear God, get back to me as soon as humanly possible. Something truly awful is going to occur today in Dallas today and I don't know what time it will happen. I don't know who else to call, Pete. I don't know who else to trust. I attempted to reach you at the offices of *The Saturday Evening Post*, but all I got was an answering machine."

It was approximately 11:30 A.M. EST when Billy's telephone rang. He answered it breathlessly.

"Pete?!"

"Yes, Billy, it's me. Are you sure?"

"Hell, I haven't had one that didn't come true yet, Pete. What the hell do I do?!"

"Just hang tight. I'll attempt to reach Secret Service. I've already tried the White House to no avail. Shit, even I'm not sure what to tell them if I reach them, Billy. If I get through, I'll do everything in my power to keep you anonymous. Damn, how do we do this? I don't want to endanger you or anyone else, Billy."

"Pete, we're talking about the President of the United States. If you have to divulge your source, it's all right. I can live with it."

All communications to the White House and the Secret Service were shut down on that fateful day. Pete Hamill never got through, so additional conspiracy theories abound. Later on, Pete Hamill consoled Billy over the telephone, as Billy wept openly.

The JFK assassination, which affected all people who lived through it, in so many ways, forever altered lives. It was truly the end of the age of innocence.

Billy asked his older, but still young friend.

"Pete, can one change the future?"

"Billy, I'm not certain we can change the present."

Chapter Eleven

After over two years abroad, Pete Hamill left his job with *The Saturday Evening Post* and returned to the United States in order to resume his journalistic career with the *New York Post*. Pete had dearly missed his home in New York City and longed for the daily excitement in the greatest city in the world, despite all of its warts.

One of the first people Hamill contacted upon his returning was his younger friend Billy Farrell. It was late 1965 and the world had changed, and not for the better. Billy, now twenty years of age, was now in his senior year of college at NYU and had already passed the computer based test and physical ability test in order to become a NYC Firefighter. However, he would have to wait until he fulfilled the requirement of being twenty-one years old in order to join. Meanwhile, he furthered his education.

Billy continued to have dreams about the beautiful dark-haired girl with the round face. He began to have serious doubts as to whether or not he'd ever meet her and on occasion, if she actually existed.

Meanwhile, his friend, Pete Hamill, was building a reputation as a great columnist with the *New York Post*. There were thousands of New York City inhabitants who would await Hamill's daily columns with the same eager anticipation of watching their favorite ballplayers and theatrical stars. Hamill's columns were topical, controversial, and hard hitting in their impact and often brutal honesty. Hamill did not pull any of his punches.

Billy's visions of the dark-haired girl persisted, as her visage would now appear to him nightly. She was astoundingly beautiful, he thought. He wondered if he would ever actually meet her.

When Billy turned twenty-one years of age in February of 1966, he joined the ranks of the FDNY. He had achieved his goal of being a firefighter. Now that Billy was a man, Pete Hamill invited him to go drinking with him to various NYC watering holes and in the process, Billy, still addicted to great journalism, met some of the most extraordinary writers of the era. Hamill introduced him to George Kimball, who had been nominated for a Pulitzer Prize in Journalism and was one of the more intriguing characters of his time, and to legends such as Jimmy Breslin, Dick Young, Charles Pierce, Joel Oppenheimer of the *Village Voice* and many other literary greats. All enjoyed his company, as Billy was both erudite and knowledgeable in regard to their work.

Drinking was both the enjoyment and bane of many of these gentlemen's existence. Pete Hamill's candid introspection, *A Drinking Life*, covered that subject as well as any book ever written.

Billy spent many hours with these legends at gin mills such as "The Lion's Head," a renowned Greenwich Village hangout of some of the giants of literature. As Pete Hamill wrote in *A Drinking Life*, "I don't think many New York bars ever had such a glorious mixture of newspapermen, painters, musicians, seamen, ex-communists, priests and nuns, athletes, stockbrokers, politicians and folksingers, bound together in the leveling democracy of drink."

It was at the Lion's Head that Billy and Hamill had a deep conversation about Billy's gift, if that is what it was.

"So, Pete, you told me earlier that you believe that we cannot change the future and you mentioned that you weren't even certain we could even change the present?"

"William, you mentioned that your dreams and visions were becoming more frequent. Perhaps you're the one who **CAN** change the future. Maybe some great entity has given you this gift for a reason. Have you ever given consideration to the possibility that you were chosen? After all, no one else is experiencing these images."

"I wish I knew, Pete. I'm just an average guy, a firefighter just trying to get by. Truthfully, these visions I get, they often frighten me. I mean, why me?"

"That's a conundrum, my friend. Maybe you're being prepared for something truly great, Billy."

"Pete, seriously, what could possibly be greater than the Amoros catch in '55 that saved the World Series for the Brooklyn Dodgers?!"

Pete Hamill laughed as he lifted his glass in a proposed toast. "To Sandy Amoros and the Brooklyn Dodgers!"

Pete Hamill stared down at the empty glass in his hand. His face became a serious mask.

"I can't even alter the present. I've seen what this stuff does to people, Billy. I realize I'm an alcoholic. I've seen what drink has done to my own family."

The bartender filled Pete's glass and knocked on the wooden bar with his clenched fist.

"This one's on the house, Pete."

Pete once more stared at the glass in his hand before continuing. "Billy, I'm almost afraid to ask, but have your visions included anything about my future?"

Billy smiled before responding.

"Actually, Pete, my visions seem to cease in the early twenty-first century. And for the record, you're still alive, writing and thriving."

Pete Hamill raised his glass, smiled, and replied, "Well, that at least means I made it to sixty-five! Therefore, I guess it's safe to down this drink! Here's to the accuracy of your dreams, Billy! And great luck with your career in firefighting. We need more men like you!"

The two great friends downed their beverages.

Chapter Twelve

It was Pete Hamill who saw her first. In 1967, Pete had made a trip to Paris to write a piece about a jazz musician for *Esquire* Magazine. On the evening before his flight home to the U.S., Hamill was invited to an exhibition of gymnastics at the Palais Des Sports. Hamill's seats were approximately seventy-five feet from the athletes and he had a clear view of the competitors. Various sports were represented, but it was the women's tumbling competition that captured his attention.

The crowd grew suddenly excited upon hearing the introduction of one of the participants, a Jennifer Swanson from Illinois in the United States. While full-bodied tumblers competed, without warning, a wheelchair emerged from one of the tunnels leading to the arena. Pete saw the young woman exit the wheelchair; he could only view her peripherally until she turned and faced him. Pete thought to himself, "I've seen her face, but where?"

Then he noticed for the initial time that the young lady was legless. At once, he recalled exactly where he had seen her face. His friend, the NYPD's sketch artist Ed Barrow, had drawn her face based on the description given to him by Billy Farrell! He had found the girl of his friend's dreams! She truly exists, just as did all of the others in Billy's dreams.

Here she was competing successfully against full-bodied young women. Then Pete saw what was evident in the artist's sketch, which was implausibly accurate. Jennifer Swanson was stunningly beautiful. Jennifer won the event with an incredible exhibition of power tumbling, but all Pete could think of was his excitement over the prospect of telling Billy that he had found the girl of his dreams. She was real and she was beyond inspirational and lovely.

Prophet's End

Pete made it a point to visit the young woman after the event was over. He decided to not inform her of his friend's dreams about her. Pete reasoned that it would somehow work out in some sort of natural process and not by informing her of a seemingly preposterous vision. Pete Hamill knew exactly what to ask her. "Jennifer, do you have plans of performing in the United States?" Jennifer flashed a brilliant smile and replied.

"Yes, in fact I'll be in New York City next week, at Madison Square Garden."

Chapter Thirteen

Upon arriving back at Kennedy Airport, Pete dialed Billy's telephone number excitedly. Billy answered and spoke first.

"You saw her! You met her!"

"How in hell did you know?!"

Billy laughed before responding.

"How do you think?"

"Oh, my God, you had another dream!"

"It was vivid, Pete. I even saw you there."

Billy paused before continuing.

"In the dream, Pete, you introduced us at Madison Square Garden. Therefore, I fully expect you to attend the event with me on Friday evening."

"Billy, I'd be honored. Damn, am I in the Twilight Zone, or what?"

"I think we all are, Pete. Hey, I hope she likes me."

"Wait, Billy, how can she not like you? She's going to marry you, right?"

Billy laughed.

"At least that's what was in my dream, but Pete, other than the church altar vision and seeing her visage on countless occasions, I've never spoken to her or heard her speak to me. I'm nervous as all hell."

"Just let nature take its course."

Pete hesitated before asking.

"Billy, you've seen her body, right? I mean, in the dream last evening, you saw more than just her face, right?"

"You mean the legless part? Pete, we've met so many brainless people, why not marry a beautiful legless girl?"

"I can't believe you're talking about marrying a girl you haven't met!"

Prophet's End

"Pete, do you ever think your life would have been less weird if I never showed up at your office in 1961?"

"We live in New York City, my friend, we live and breathe weirdness. It is an integral part of our existence."

Chapter Fourteen

Billy's heart was palpitating as he entered the main entrance of Madison Square Garden on Eighth Avenue and 50th Street. It would be the last year of the old Garden, as the new Garden would open in 1968. Pete Hamill decided to cover the event for the *New York Post*. It was just another excuse concocted in order to introduce Billy to Jennifer Swanson.

Many of those in attendance were not well versed or educated in the nuances of gymnastics, however, when they saw Jennifer introduced as a participant, they all cheered wildly. New Yorkers are renowned for being champions of the underdogs. Therefore, seeing Jennifer in her wheelchair elicited an extremely warm and favorable response. Little did the majority of the crowd realize that Jennifer was considered one of the more accomplished of the competitors.

One can only begin to imagine what was going through Billy's mind as he anticipated the alleged inevitable. Here he was, about to meet a young woman who had dominated his dreams since the age of six. Now, at twenty-two years of age and a grown man, he began to doubt his sanity. After all, he had actually dreamed that this was to be his wife. How can any sentient being rationalize the absurdity of such a possibility? What if she wasn't even remotely attracted to him? However, everything else he had visions of came to be reality.

And then another logical thought came to him. What would he say to her? Does she actually already KNOW him? I mean, why else, did she invariably appear in his dreams. Did she plan this? Is this some sort of diabolical scheme and if so, who is the author of such a plot?

Billy's emotions ran the full gamut. There was excitement, fear, dread, anticipation, wonderment, confusion, and a sense of the absurd. Was there a grander scheme involved? Was this some sort of a master plan drawn up by some higher entity? Billy was raised a devout Catholic, however, this seemed like nothing he'd ever heard in his upbringing.

One brief thought invading Billy's thoughts was that of the possibility of Jennifer being malevolent. Did she have any connection whatsoever to the outcome of his dreams? After all, there was the horrific vision of JFK's assassination. However, Billy then thought of Sandy Amoros's incredible catch vision. Certainly, there was no malice in that.

The arrival of Pete Hamill on the floor of Madison Square Garden more than slightly assuaged Billy's apprehension and fear. Pete glanced up at Billy in his seat at "courtside" and smiled. Billy nodded and shrugged his shoulders which elicited a laugh from Hamill. Pete attempted to imagine what Billy was feeling, but of course, knowingly fell considerably short.

Prior to her performance, Jennifer's arrival in her wheelchair was met with significant applause from the crowd. As Jennifer climbed out of her seat and onto the mat she would be competing on, Billy saw at once her beautiful round face and any thoughts of her perhaps being malevolent vanished from his mind. Billy thought Jennifer was the most beautiful girl he had ever seen and thought it surreal that the girl who had invaded his dreams actually existed.

Near the conclusion of the show, Pete signaled for Billy to join him on the floor of Madison Square Garden. Hamill spoke briefly with a security guard who allowed Billy to enter. Pete led Billy to a tunnel which led to the area where the competitors had gathered to meet the media.

"Are you all right, Buddy?"

Billy laughed before responding.

"I guess I'm as good as I'm going to be considering I'm a participant in some sort of mystical dream. This is akin to an out-of-body experience, I would imagine. It's as if I'm watching myself."

Jennifer Swanson was concluding an interview with a WINS reporter as Pete and Billy approached. At once, she recognized Pete, who she had met the prior week in Paris. Jennifer smiled and extended her hand to Pete and spoke.

"It's Pete, right? It's nice to see you again."

Jennifer had yet to notice Billy who stood a mere five feet away and slightly behind the beauty's wheelchair.

Jennifer continued, "Did you enjoy the show? I goofed on one of my tumbles."

Jennifer giggled as Pete responded.

"I loved the show, Jennifer, but I can fit what I know about your sport on the head of a pin. I apologize if that offends you."

Jennifer giggled once more, a chuckle which tugged at Billy's heartstrings. He loved her voice.

"I'm not offended at all. I'm just pleased you enjoyed watching. Oh, and call me Jen. My friends call me Jen."

Pete Hamill placed his hand on Jennifer's shoulder before replying. "All right then, Jen it is. Jen, I'd like to introduce you to a dear friend of mine, Billy Farrell."

Jennifer turned slightly to her left and upon seeing Billy for the initial time, her facial expression changed completely. Although her smile dissipated, she appeared slightly perplexed, as if she were attempting to determine what or who she was looking at.

"Do I know you? Have we met?"

Billy had no idea how to respond. He briefly searched in his mind for the proper response. Finally, he settled for what he hoped would suffice. He was not about to inform her that she occupied his dreams for nearly two decades.

"I doubt it. I would have remembered someone as astoundingly lovely as you."

Jennifer blushed and giggled before responding.

Prophet's End

"You really do look familiar. Perhaps I saw you in a dream." Jennifer's reaction caught Billy entirely off guard. It was the last thing he'd expected. It jolted him to his core.

Jennifer noticed the fact that Billy seemed suddenly impacted, but did not associate the affect with what she had said.

"Are you all right, Billy? You seem a bit shaken."

Billy attempted to regain his composure; however, although in perfectly excellent health, he suddenly collapsed onto the floor.

Chapter Fifteen

As Billy lay in his bed at Lenox Hill Hospital in Manhattan, he began to flutter his eyelids. As he became cognizant of his surroundings, he immediately saw Pete Hamill seated next to his bed.

"You're going to be okay, Ace, but you gave us all a scare. All your tests came back negative, especially the one on your brain."

Billy laughed and asked how long he'd been there.

"Just a few hours and you'll be released first thing in the morning. They're just holding you for observation."

Pete peered briefly over his shoulder before continuing. Well, I'm going to call it a night. I've got to show up at the *New York Post* offices in the morning, but you're not going to be alone for long. You have a visitor."

Billy straightened up in his bed and peered towards the door as Jennifer Swanson wheeled herself into the room. Jen smiled sweetly before remarking.

"You're not going to faint on me again, are you? You're about to give me some sort of complex. Do I have that affect on you?"

Jen's giggle made Billy tingle.

"No, I promise not to keel over again. Gosh, I'm so sorry I ruined your evening. The only effect you have on me is the fact you're extraordinarily beautiful."

Jen giggled before replying.

"Well, in that case, you should ask me out on a date."

Billy's next thought was the dream in which he lifted her veil at the church altar and saw her beautiful face in his wondrous dream.

"Will you go out with me, Jen?"

"Yeah, yes I will. I'd like that very much."

Prophet's End

Billy and Jennifer stared into each other's eyes for several moments before Jen broke the silence.

"Are you certain we've never met before, Billy?"

"Actually, Jen, I'm not that clear. Perhaps in that dream you mentioned."

Jen reached for Billy's hand and held it tightly.

"Billy, what do you do?" Our conversation at Madison Square Garden was interrupted by some guy fainting.

"I'm just a firefighter, Jen."

Jen giggled before jokingly scolding.

"Just? Just?! Just a firefighter? You're a hero, Billy. You save lives and protect us."

Less than a year later, Billy and Jen were married and another of Billy's dreams bore fruition. Billy reenacted the scene in his dream when he lifted Jen's veil and embellished it by kissing her beautiful round face.

The young couple settled in Billy and Pete's beloved New York City.

Chapter Sixteen

Following his marriage to beautiful Jen, although Billy ceased dreaming about her, his other visions increased in volume and intensity. There were frequent dreams of happenings in and around New York City, and with his friend, Pete, making occasional sojourns to Vietnam where he covered the unpopular war, Billy was sure to remind his friend that he had visions of Pete alive and well and writing in the early twenty-first century. Not that Hamill would have been influenced by danger as he had become one of the leading journalistic voices against what he considered an unjust war. Pete had literally been added to "An Enemies List" of Richard Nixon's White House, part of a group of journalists, performers, celebrities, and other media people who were opposed to the war. However, Billy made sure to report all of his visions to Pete because of the fact that he seemed more concerned about his friend's well being than he was. As Pete reported from his many journeys to Vietnam, "I discovered I wasn't afraid of death."

In April of 1969, Billy experienced another vivid dream about baseball. This time it revolved around the New York Mets, the perpetual doormat of the National League and the laughing stock of baseball. The Mets, nearly always finishing in last place, were expected to be slightly improved in 1969, but certainly not a playoff contender and most definitely not a World Series winner, but that is what Billy dreamed. Not only did Billy's vision include a trip to the fall classic, but a World Series victory versus the formidable American powerhouse, the Baltimore Orioles.

When Pete was alerted of what was to occur with the Mets later that season, he reasoned that Billy's clairvoyance had sprung a leak. "It's time to get a lube job for your brain, William."

Prophet's End

However, led by former 1955 Brooklyn Dodgers superstar Gil Hodges as their manager, the Mets behind an array of outstanding young pitchers and an unlikely blend of veteran players and untested youngsters, managed to win both the pennant and the World Series. Both Pete and Billy wondered aloud when exactly these dreams would finally conclude. And despite the fact that Billy was deeply in love with Jen, he decided never to tell her of his visions or the fact that she dominated them for so many years.

In the late '60s, Billy and Jennifer welcomed their two children into the world, Peter, named after Hamill, and Angela, named after African American civil rights activist, Angela Davis. The kids grew to be intelligent, thoughtful and attractive children. Life was perfect, and despite having a few close calls while firefighting, Billy, having been given commendations for bravery on three occasions, managed to escape with minor abrasions and injuries.

Chapter Seventeen

By 1977, Billy and Jen had the perfect marriage and resided in an East Greenwich Village flat with their children, Peter, eight, and Angela, six. Billy had recently been promoted from Lieutenant to the rank of Captain, and his popularity with his co-workers made him a strong candidate for the eventual position of Battalion Chief.

One Friday during the school year of 1977, Angela, the younger of the siblings, arrived home from school in tears. Peter, her slightly older brother's entrance was also troubling. Peter entered the house sporting a black eye; his shirt was ripped and his knuckles were scraped. Upon seeing her kids in disarray, Jen immediately followed them to their rooms and asked what had occurred and if they were all right.

Peter responded that he was fine and that he didn't want to talk about it and little Angela just nodded her head as Jen attempted successfully to stifle her tears by holding her. After Angela had calmed down, Jen took both children into the bathroom in order to tend to them. After drying Angela's tears and applying a damp washcloth to the insignificant injuries suffered by Peter, she fed the children their dinner and sent them to their rooms to watch television. Jen would send Billy in to investigate once he arrived home from the fire station. Angela, in particular, was extremely close with her father, and Jen reasoned correctly that he'd manage to find out what had happened. Pete Hamill, still a great friend of the family, was to be a dinner guest that evening.

When Billy arrived home early that evening, Jen advised him of the situation. Billy's initial stop was to see his daughter, Angela, since he was aware that his son, Peter, was often too proud to confide any possible weaknesses, emotionally or physically. In Little League baseball, Billy once watched as Peter took a hard pitch to his wrist from a hard-throwing wild left-handed pitcher and he noted that his brave son absolutely refused medical attention and fought back tears.

Upon entering Angela's room, Billy asked, "Are you all right, Princess?"

Angela replied by shaking her head affirmatively, but not speaking. "I'll be right back, angel. Everything will be all right."

Angela smiled and Billy left the room.

Billy entered Peter's room and gently said, "That's quite a shiner you've got there, son. I'm sort of hoping that the other guy looks worse."

"I got in a few shots, Dad."

Billy smiled and responded. "I hope you had a good reason, son."

"I did, Dad, honest."

"I believe you, Peter."

Billy then re-entered Angela's room and sat down next to her on her bed. On Angela's wall was a large photograph of her mom tumbling in an exhibition and another of her mom high up in the air in an acrobatic pose.

"Do you want to talk about it, sweetheart?"

Angela, a little round-faced pretty brunette, reminiscent of the visage of her mom who appeared in Billy's dreams years ago, slowly shook her head negatively.

Billy kissed his daughter's forehead and spoke softly.

"If you tell me why you were so upset, angel, I'm not promising I can fix it, but I cannot even try if I don't know what it is. I promise to do anything I can to make you feel better. It really bothers me whenever you cry, honey. No matter what it was that upset you, Mommy and Daddy love you very much."

With that, little Angela began sobbing once more. Suddenly, Angela blurted out, "Mikey said that Mommy was a freak! He called her half a mommy!"

Billy held Angela in his arms.

"Angela, sweetheart, your mommy is the greatest and most beautiful mommy in the entire world. She's a champion, too. She can do more things than anyone else's mommy. And I love both of you with all my heart. It doesn't matter what mean people say, Angela. They're just words and words cannot hurt us. Now, give me a big hug and a smile, Princess."

Angela leaped out of her bed and into her father's arms. Billy pointed to the photos of Jen on the walls.

"Look at your mommy. She's a great athlete and she's the most beautiful mommy in the whole universe. I'd like to see Mikey's mother even attempt to do what Mommy can do!"

Billy hesitated before continuing.

"Don't let anyone's words ever hurt you, Princess. Okay?"

"Okay, Daddy, I'll try."

"Good. Do you know what happened to your brother?"

"Yeah, Daddy, but please don't be angry with him. He beat Mikey up."

Billy smiled before responding.

"I promise not to be angry with Peter, angel. I don't like for either of you to fight, but it sure sounds as if Mikey had it coming to him. Sleep well, Princess. And if any of the kids ever says anything mean to you, just tell me, okay?"

Angela smiled and answered, "Okay, Daddy, I love you!"

"I love you, Princess!"

Chapter Eighteen

Pete Hamill arrived for dinner at 7:00 P.M. He had just completed his latest novel, *Flesh and Blood*, about the brutality of boxing. The *New York Times* review stated, "*A taut, punchy read. Hamill writes stark, staccato sentences designed to sting, building suspense that is rooted in character... Makes "Rocky" seem like a fairy tale.*" Pete Hamill was clearly at the top of his game.

At dinner that evening, Billy, Jen and Hamill discussed poor Angela's ordeal at school earlier that day. Hamill also smiled as he was made aware of how her older brother, Peter, came to his sister's defense against a larger child.

"He apparently acquitted himself quite well, especially when considering the abrasions on his knuckles. You not only named him after me, but it appears as if your son has inherited some of my earlier traits."

Billy laughed uproariously before responding.

"Earlier traits? I seem to recall seeing someone who looked exactly like you get into a brawl at ringside just a short while ago!" (Hamill indeed, was involved in a melee at ringside, one in which he pounded out six thugs with thunderous left hooks after the men had made untoward remarks about a lovely Puerto Rican woman seated at ringside. The woman, Ramona Negron, was at the time the girlfriend of the great boxer, Jose "Chegui" Torres, a dear and close personal friend of Hamill's. Hamill would eventually marry Ramona. They have since divorced.)

Pete winced before replying.

"Touché! Guilty as charged."

Pete Hamill then changed his expression to one of seriousness. "You know, humiliation, and that's what it was for both little Angela and Billy, can persuade you to commit semi-violent acts. Your kids are too young to fully understand how unimaginably great their mom is."

Jen sat straight up and replied, "Aw, I'm blushing. Thanks, Pete."

Pete continued, "Hell, I've even retaliated with hurtful and venomous words in my columns and more often than I'd like to admit. It's a method I developed in the streets of Brooklyn growing up."

Billy replied after shaking his head, "Pete, the great majority of the people you verbally assault had it coming. There is nothing wrong with being sensitive to injustice."

"Thanks, William, but on occasion I've actually regretted some of the things I've written. Keep in mind that the printed word really cannot be retracted. You can apologize in print, but folks will only remember the original words. Printed words are permanent."

Jen immediately replied, "Yes, but in your case, Pete, you're building an enormously great legacy of being fair and open-minded. No one can be 100 percent perfect. Not even you."

Pete Hamill took a sip of the drink in his hand before responding. "Thanks, Jen, but you guys are a bit biased. The humiliation that both Angela and Peter suffered today will only make them stronger. You know, I grew up in a state of rage. My mom, Anne, and my dad, Bill, were poor. I loved my mother dearly and I grew to respect my dad, eventually. I would explode into violence, (from "Irrational Ravings" by Pete Hamill, G.P. Putnam's Sons, 1971) my hands clenched into fists, hammering and battering at people I did not even know. The violence was always white and blind and savage, and when I think about the cause of it now, it always seemed to involve humiliation. I remember one cold winter afternoon when I was fourteen. I had won a scholarship to a Jesuit high school called Regis, which was a long subway ride from Brooklyn. Most of the students were upper middle class, and I spent the first few months there in a state of desperate unhappiness. I imagined Regis as a place where older boys shared a democratic camaraderie with younger boys, where you learned from one another. Instead, I found a place stinking with class rank and privilege and a student body that was, in retrospect, docile and cliquish. One rainy winter day, I arrived at school soaked by the walk from Lexington Avenue. There were large holes in the bottom of my shoes. I did not own a pair of galoshes; instead, cardboard had been stuffed into the shoes. When I went into the locker room, my shoes were squishing with rainwater. I found a piece of cardboard in a wastebasket and sat down on a bench and took my shoes off. I was tearing the cardboard to fit the shoes when I heard laughter. I looked up to see a couple of juniors snickering and giggling at my shoes. I felt humiliated and grubby and helpless. I sat in class like a bomb, and when school was over, I waited down the street in the rain in a doorway on Park Avenue, until I saw one of the young men who had laughed. I exploded in a fury of punching, kicking, and stomping and left the kid smashed and bleeding on the sidewalk, before I ran off in the rain. I didn't go to school for two days, because I was frightened and somehow ashamed. Ever since, it has been impossible for me to watch a black kid walk into a white school without wondering if he had cardboard in his shoes. Ever since, I've been afraid of the murderer who lives in my body."

Both Billy and Jen sat enthralled as Pete Hamill continued.

"But there was more to the anger than poverty. There was something in me that wanted the world to be fair. I grew up hearing stories of the injustices in Northern Ireland, where my folks were from. There were stories of what the Protestant landlords were doing to Catholic AND Protestant workers. That led to a kind of rude sympathy for underdogs, for blacks, Puerto Ricans and Indians, for the damaged and the lost, which was further deepened by the fact that as a young man in America my father had lost a leg playing soccer. In the years when I was growing up, my father had a street fighter's sense of bigotry; he wouldn't let anyone use the words 'nigger' or 'spic' in the house, and once, when I was about eleven, I used the word 'kike' at the dinner table, and he leaned over and smacked my face brutally and said,

53

'Benny Leonard was a kike.' I didn't know that Benny Leonard was a Jew off the Lower East Side who had become the greatest of all lightweight champions of the world, but I never used the word 'kike' again. It is a simple matter to sneer at that story, at its lack of sophistication or its possibly patronizing implications. But it was the way you learned things in that neighborhood, and I thank the old man for doing what he did. He would never have described himself as 'liberal.' He simply hated unfairness, bigotry, and the absence of justice."

Jen smiled as she refilled Pete Hamill's glass before responding. "Wow, perhaps I can convince you to have a long talk with the kids."

Pete Hamill laughed and retorted.

"Thanks, however, I strongly suspect, actually I *know*, that you will handle it perfectly, just as you manage everything else in your lives."

Pete then concluded with.

"Just know this; I truly feel empathy for both little Peter and Angela. But having parents like you and Billy, I know they're in the greatest of hands."

Chapter Nineteen

On the morning of November 24, 1971, Pete Hamill answered his phone to hear Billy laughing hysterically. Between guffaws, Billy managed to compose himself in order to be slightly less unintelligible.

"Pete, this one you're not going to believe!"

"What, did Spiro Agnew utter something intelligent?"

"Pete, this one's a beauty! This is the weirdest dream I've ever had. I have never laughed so hard in my life. I hope you're sitting down, because this one is so implausible, it's entirely absurd. Mel Brooks couldn't have created this spectacle. A plane is going to be hijacked today."

Pete hesitated before responding.

"And this is supposed to be funny?"

"Wait, you've got to hear this, Pete. It was as vivid a dream as I've ever had. It was as if I was aboard the plane! Don't worry, no one gets hurt. Not only that, the dream included the future. This guy, the hijacker becomes a hero! A folk hero. There will be books and songs written about him."

"So, I shouldn't alert the authorities?"

"Pete, honest, I wouldn't. Besides, not only doesn't anyone get hurt, but even the people onboard won't know they're in any imminent danger. Hell, again, if we alerted the authorities, I'd be found out and who is going to believe that I can see the future. I'd be arrested for complicity in the skyjacking. I mean, how in hell would I know about it in advance? Besides, I don't want this guy to get caught, and he won't! Not now, not ever!"

Pete sighed, laughed and replied.

"I'm all ears. This may be the weirdest yet."

"Pete, you don't know the half of it. Get this, some schmegeggie named Dan Cooper is going to purchase an airline ticket in order to fly from Portland to Seattle. It's Flight #305 on a Boeing 727. It's got thirty-six people on board."

Pete laughed.

"You're beginning to frighten me, Billy."

"Get this, this Dan Cooper guy, and that's not his real name, no one will ever find out his real name, purchases this one way ticket at Northeast Orient's counter at the airport in Portland. He gets on the plane and is seated in the back of the passenger cabin in seat #18C. He lights a cigarette and orders a bourbon and soda."

Pete Hamill is now laughing so hard that he is practically convulsing. "Wait, you dreamed all of these minute details and you don't even know his real name?! You even know his seat number, but your vision didn't include the guy's actual name? Billy, I think your dream apparatus has finally imploded."

"Hear me out, this is hilarious. This Cooper guy, or whoever he is, passes a note to a flight attendant named Florence Schaffner, a real attractive doll."

"Billy, this is insane. You know the name of the flight attendant, but not the hijacker?!"

Billy laughs before continuing.

"Well, 'Cooper' passes her this note at just after 2:50 P.M., moments after the flight takes off. This Florence gal, remember she's hot, thinks he's flirting with her, so she shoves it in her purse without looking at it."

"You've really lost it this time, Billy."

"Well, 'Cooper' whispers to her, 'Miss, you'd better look at that note. I have a bomb.' It's supposedly in his briefcase. The note is all in upper case neatly printed letters. He motions to her to sit down next to him, the flight is not full, and he dictates his demands to her. He wants $200,000 in unmarked negotiable U.S. currency. (That would be equivalent to well over a million dollars today) So, this Florence gal takes the note up to the cockpit and when she returns to Cooper, he is wearing dark sunglasses."

"Jesus, Billy, did you dream this in wide screen?!

Hamill is laughing.

"So, the pilot, some guy named William Scott, notifies Seattle-Tacoma Airport air traffic control, which in turn informs local and federal authorities."

Hamill laughs again.

"You even dreamed the pilot's name!"

"As I said, this was the most vivid dream to date, Pete. Now, this D.B. Cooper guy"

Pete interrupts.

"I thought you didn't know his name. D.B. Cooper?"

"Oh, that's another thing. Due to some News media communication error, his name was transcribed as 'D.B. Cooper.'"

Pete is now beside himself with laughter.

"Oh, sure, blame the media! It's my fault!"

"So, Cooper tells Florence to instruct the pilot to inform the passengers that everything is all right. The pilot makes an announcement that their arrival in Seattle would be delayed because of some "minor mechanical difficulty. Cooper is polite, calm, and well spoken. Cooper has demanded the $200,000 and a parachute. The aircraft circles Puget Sound for approximately two hours to allow Seattle police and the FBI to assemble Cooper's parachute and ransom money and to mobilize emergency personnel."

"You're serious, Billy, this Cooper is going to get away with it!"

"Yes, isn't it delicious? Cooper actually orders another bourbon and water and attempts to give this Florence gal the change!"

"Don't tell me, she cannot accept because of airline regulations!"

"Yes, yes!! Isn't this great? Well, Cooper demands 10,000 unmarked $20 bills, but he rejects the military issue parachute offered by McChord Air Force Base. The plane has now landed in Seattle.

Cooper insists on civilian parachutes with manually operated rip chords."

Pete laughs and replies.

"Brilliant!"

"Well, Seattle police get the parachutes from a local skydiving school. Once the delivery is completed, Cooper allows all passengers, Florence and the other flight attendant, Alice Hancock, to exit the plane. Donald Nyrop, Northeast Orient's president, authorizes the payment of the ransom and ordered all employees to fully cooperate with Cooper. At 7.40 P.M., the plane takes off with Cooper, the pilot William Scott, a flight attendant named Mucklow, co-pilot Rataczak, and flight engineer H.E. Anderson aboard."

"Jesus, Billy, you've got me rooting for this guy, Cooper!"

"Well, while they were refueling on the runway, Cooper tells the entire crew to enter the cockpit and close the door. At 8:13 P.M., the aircraft's tail section sustains a sudden upward movement."

Pete reacts excitedly.

"Don't tell me, the SOB parachuted!"

"Yes, yes!!!! The crazy bastard is wearing a business suit and he's got the cash in a knapsack! But my dream doesn't end. It extends to the very beginning of the twenty-first century. Like I said, Pete, all my dreams seem to stop there. Well, Cooper, or whatever his name is, gets away with it. There are songs written about him."

"Billy, if this comes true, I may write a song about him!"

Billy laughs before concluding.

"Well, of course, there's an extensive FBI manhunt. The plane was headed to Mexico City according to Cooper's commands, but he bailed out somewhere in the Pacific Northwest. The FBI conducts this lengthy investigation and I believe it was still ongoing entering the twenty-first century. And get this, they stated that the perpetrator, and they never actually learned his actual name, had never been located or identified. At one time the FBI surmised he didn't survive his jump, but neither the parachute nor the cash was ever found."

"Billy, I'll be glued to the news reports today."

Pete's demeanor changed briefly to being serious.

"William, did you ever consider undergoing some sort of neurological testing?"

"Actually, I have, Pete, but I honestly fear that if the CIA ever became aware of this curse, or gift, or whatever it is I have, they'd most likely lock me in a room somewhere and use me for nefarious reasons. They'd most likely claim I had disappeared."

"I agree, Billy, this will have to remain a secret for our entire lives, I suppose."

Later that day, Pete Hamill while watching the news reports, sat there in disbelief as the exact events that Billy foretold, became reality. Pete headed to "Rattigan's Bar" to get sufficiently inebriated. He drank numerous toasts to "D.B. Cooper."

Chapter Twenty

Following little Angela's humiliating experience in grade school, the one in which she came home sobbing because an older boy had made fun of her mom, neither Billy or Jen were aware of any additional incidents regarding her physical appearance.

Jen had been born with the condition, a birth defect that was unexplainable. However, having no legs never deterred Jen from living a full and remarkable life. She was otherworldly beautiful, had competed successfully versus full-bodied athletes, and, of course, was raising a family of her own with absolutely zero difficulty. Jennifer Farrell, nee Jennifer Swanson, was inspirational beyond belief. Peter, now eighteen years of age in the year 1987, was particularly proud of his mother's accomplishments and extremely protective of her image. Peter, with hope of being a law enforcement officer, was also highly protective of his lovely little sister, Angela, now sixteen and in high school. Peter would actually ask his mom various questions about her youth and how she coped with the seeming disadvantage of having no legs. Jen would always answer truthfully, that since she was born with the condition, it posed no hindrance whatsoever, and that if she had to live life over again, she'd remain legless. Jen was, of course, speaking the truth.

Angela, a bit more reserved than her older brother, would never discuss her mom's alleged physical disability with her or anyone else, for that matter. Angela never brought any of her friends over to the house and often Jen would wonder if it were because of the humiliation she suffered when the older boy had made cruel remarks about her condition. Not wanting to press the subject that Jen reasoned may result in emotional distress for her daughter, Jen never brought the matter up.

Prophet's End

Angela's closest friend in high school was Sharon Carswell, an absolutely stunning sixteen-year-old African American girl. Sharon was not only beautiful, but she was the most popular girl in Angela's classes. Sharon, seemingly near perfect, was a great student and admired by all of her classmates and teachers. Her beauty combined with her ebullience made her the apple of everyone's eye. Sharon had no enemies on the planet.

One day, in the midst of her junior year, Sharon, however, was involved in a horrific car crash. Although injuries were suffered by both her parents and younger brother, Sharon's injuries were the most significant. Sharon lie in a hospital for several weeks and her life hung in the balance. Sharon eventually pulled through, however, her left leg, which had been pinned and crushed in the accident, had to be amputated. Sharon's young world had shattered, and although she had been fitted for a prosthetic, she was having an enormously difficult time in dealing with her misfortune; she was disconsolate. Sharon, an honor student, was also a tremendous athlete, a captain of both the volleyball team and a track and field star.

Angela was extremely concerned as her closest friend became withdrawn to the point of being almost a recluse. Sharon, normally a great student, would just go through the motions in class as if she were merely fulfilling an obligation, her demeanor being doleful. Sharon normally would participate and often be the leader of various school organizations, but now, after classes concluded, she would immediately go home with nary a word to anyone. Angela had lost her best friend and confidante. Both young ladies, super intelligent and thoughtful, were inseparable. Inseparable, that is, until the life-altering calamity.

Jen, of course, had heard about the catastrophe; it had been all over the news; however, with her daughter being independent and not given to sharing her innermost thoughts, really had no idea how well she knew her classmate.

"Angela, how well do you know the poor girl involved in the car crash the other day?"

Angela answered, a bit surprised that her mother would ask, since the teenager had never invited any of her classmates to their home. "Fairly well, Mom."

Of course, the answer was an understatement as Angela and Sharon were practically sisters and partook in a camaraderie that few share.

Angela not only grieved for Sharon's loss of self esteem, her sudden lack of confidence, and realized that she was not only losing her dearest friend, but also arrived at the conclusion that Sharon was losing herself, her wonderful persona and demeanor unrecognizable with little or no association with her past. Sharon had packed it in, quit on life, as it were.

One night, upon arriving home from school, Angela lay in bed and began to cry, lamenting the loss of her once great friend and empathizing with what she must feel. Then suddenly she thought of her mom, Jen.

A great revelation struck Angela as if it were a lightning bolt. Her mom, her wonderful mom! Never once had she seen her mom depressed, angry or even remotely upset about her condition. Never once did her mom discuss with her what it was like to have people staring at her in pity, sorrow, or wonder. No, her mom had the greatest disposition in the universe; she wore her "disability" as if it weren't, and therefore, it was not a disability or defect, it was a badge of honor. Angela's mom was perfect, she thought, and she was right. Angela immediately put in motion a plan to reclaim her best friend. She would not tell her mom about it; she would not have to, she reasoned.

Chapter Twenty-One

Following school one afternoon, Angela approached Sharon and asked if she would come over for dinner that evening. Sharon, withdrawn and now suspicious, hesitated before responding. Sharon, of course, had never even seen Angela's mom, Jen, and was entirely unaware of the fact that her friend's mother had been born with a significant birth defect.

"No, thanks, Angie, I'm going home to read."

Angela sensed the insincerity in Sharon's voice and knew that her friend was merely avoiding her, as she avoided everyone else since her misfortune.

"Sharon, I really need your help. I'm having problems with calculus."

Angela had come up with a terrific white lie. In truth, Angela had struggled briefly with calculus, a subject much like all the others which Sharon had mastered from day one.

"I suppose, Angie. If you really need me."

Angela telephoned her mom and told her that a friend of hers would be joining them for dinner. Angela, of course, did not volunteer the name of her friend and Jen, respecting her daughter's privacy, did not inquire of the identity. However, upon seeing Sharon Carswell enter through the door, walking a bit unevenly on her prosthetic, Jen immediately ascertained who she was.

"Hi, Mom, this is my friend Sharon. She's going to help me with my calculus and have dinner with us."

Sharon at once noticed that Jen's mom, who was wheeling around the kitchen, had no legs. Sharon's mouth was agape although she wasn't aware of it. Sharon immediately noticed Jen's immense beauty and warmth.

"Welcome to our home, Sharon. Gosh, you're pretty!"

Sharon shyly thanked Angela's mom and replied, "Thanks, Mrs. Farrell. You're beautiful!"

Jen giggled before responding.

"Thanks, but I really think you're ridiculously attractive. I hope you like macaroni and cheese."

Sharon, smiling for the initial time in months, became animated and appeared to almost her ebullient self.

"I love macaroni and cheese!"

Before the evening was done, Sharon was enthralled at learning that her best friend's mom had been a gifted athlete who had successfully competed against full bodied women. Sharon viewed the photographs of Jen in amazement and wonder. Angela had regained her friend and Sharon began to emerge from her shell and return to being her outgoing and beloved self. Sharon became a regular guest at the Farrell's home and returned to class with a renewed outlook on life. Soon she would develop a self-deprecating personality and began telling jokes about her condition.

Sharon would go on to study law at Columbia University and went on to become a successful Corporate Law Attorney. To this day, she and Angela remain close friends.

Chapter Twenty-Two

Sometimes the most terrible thing of all is to confirm what you have only imagined. – Pete Hamill

The decade of the 1980s was perhaps the most significant bridge between the world of the Baby Boomers' universe and what is widely considered "modern times." Although the decade saw great socioeconomic change due to advances in technology, it also ushered in that very same technology rendering our planet a much more perilous place.

The decade also heralded in the deadly AIDS epidemic, which would kill over 39 million people by the year 2013. Global warming became known to both the scientific and political community. However, perhaps even a greater concern was the survival of the human species on a more immediate level. The worldwide chasm between the haves and the have-nots actually widened to the extent that even in major metropolitan areas such as New York, homelessness reached a crisis point. Hopelessness and despair became an overwhelming factor in a multitude of lives, in both foreign and far too familiar places. One could not walk on a New York street and not see the expansive disparity between the advantaged and disadvantaged.

Terrorist attacks, although still not on the insane level of the second decade of the twenty-first century, were becoming far too frequent, and skirmishes and virtual wars in the Middle East were becoming the norm and not the exception. Extremist groups were gaining in power as serious wars broke out between fanatical religious factions, the Iran-Iraq war perhaps being the most foretelling.

It was in this world that Billy and Jen were raising their children, Peter and Angela, who became well-adjusted teenagers. By the end of the decade, Billy had now risen to the rank of Battalion Chief; however, he still looked forward to his retirement, as the days of fighting fires and rescuing people, although gratifying, were weighing on him emotionally. He had seen far too much and seen far too many lives lost and they included both the victims of infernos as well as several of his comrades.

When the year 1988 rolled around, Billy had fulfilled his twenty-two years of service for the FDNY. He had been awarded many citations and awards for bravery and had literally saved countless dozens of lives. After twenty-two years of service, a FDNY firefighter can retire regardless of his age and with full benefits. So, Billy became a civilian, which pleased both his still beautiful wife, Jen, and his son, Peter, now nineteen, and a sophomore at Columbia University, majoring in Criminology and Angela, now seventeen, and improbably as beautiful as her mom. Angela was in her junior year of high school.

Although Billy was retired from active duty, he remained close with his former compatriots and attended many of their functions and also retained a close relationship with their families. Billy, who had once considered journalism as a career, began to take English writing classes at NYU.

Meanwhile, his dear friend, Pete Hamill's career continued to flourish. Hamill, now fifty-three years of age and still ruggedly handsome and athletic, had written nine books, innumerable newspaper columns, had butted heads with countless blowhard politicians and officials, and was widely considered the greatest American columnist and one of the greatest novelists and autobiographical writers of his time.

Meantime, Billy's dreams persisted, but not as frequently as they had in earlier days. Billy was forty-three years of age and began to reassess exactly why he had been given such gifts. With more time on his hands than ever before, his prior dreams began to haunt him. He and Jen were as in love as the day they met, but she would often see Billy staring off into space, as if he were attempting to solve an age old mystery. Incredibly, he had never discussed any of his dreams with her or anyone other than Hamill, not even the dreams of her visage which had occupied his mind for his entire younger life.

Chapter Twenty-Three

The decade of the 1990s proved to be tumultuous. The Gulf War in Iraq dominated the news. In August of 1990, Iraqi forces invaded and conquered Kuwait. Oil was the most contentious consideration, as human life continued to be a non-negligible commodity. The UN condemned the action, and a coalition force led by the United States was sent to the Persian Gulf. These forces drove Iraq away from Kuwait in a mere four days. In the aftermath, the Kurds in the north and the Shiites to the south rose up in revolt. The United States eventually invaded in 2003, and Iraq was cut off from most of the world.

The first Chechen War took place between 1994-1996 between the Russian Federation and the Chechen Republic of Ichkeria. The second Chechen conflict began in 1999, and it is still ongoing.

There were genocides in Rwanda, unrest in Algeria and in the United States, race riots rocked Los Angeles. These riots resulted in 53 deaths and over 5500 property fires, and they were the result of an all-white jury acquitting four police officers of the brutal beating of a motorist named Rodney King. However, in 1993 all four police officers, three white and one Hispanic, were convicted in a federal civil rights case.

The war in Somalia commenced in 1991, and it is ongoing to this day, and in 1999, the Pakistan army overthrew the democratically elected government.

Terrorist attacks increased at an alarming rate, even here in the "safe" United States. There was the 1993 World Trade Center bombing and the bombing of a federal building in Oklahoma City in 1995, killing 168.

U.S. Naval military forces launched cruise missile attacks against Al-Qaeda bases in Afghanistan in 1998. In July of 1994, a terrorist targeting Argentina's Jewish community detonated a bomb in the AMIA headquarters killing 85 people and injuring hundreds, the deadliest bombing in Argentina history.

In January of 1998, President Bill Clinton was caught in a scandal. He was accused of having "inappropriate relations with a White House intern" (Monica Lewinsky). The U.S. House of Representatives impeached Clinton on December 19, 1998, for perjury under oath, but following an investigation by federal prosecutor Kenneth Starr, the Senate acquitted Clinton on February 12, 1999.

The world of the 1990s had become an increasingly dangerous place, and there were few, if any, safe havens.

It was in this world that Billy became even more introspective. He wanted to inform his wonderful wife, Jen, about his unusual gift, if that is what it was, and he searched for a way he could break the news to her gently. He longed to tell her of the visions of the beautiful little girl of his dreams, the one he first laid eyes on when he was six years of age, the little girl who seemed to age commensurately with him and the one he dreamed he would someday marry. He longed to tell her about dreams about things as mundane as Sandy Amoros's catch, the silliness of seeing D.B. Cooper's hijacking adventure, the chilling assassination of JFK which still haunted him, and he longed to know WHY he was chosen and the identity of who placed these visions in his mind.

After a long discussion with his dear friend Pete Hamill, Billy made a definitive decision to inform his beloved Jen of his unsolved dilemma. He prayed that this information would not dismay the love of his life in any way.

Chapter Twenty-Four

Jen's reaction was not entirely unexpected. Upon learning the extensive details of Billy's unusual and improbable bestowal, her eyes welled with tears as it appeared she was attempting to reconcile and fully comprehend and process the information she had been given. At least that was what Billy thought. He was soon to learn a shocking truth. Jen was about to reveal something perhaps even more extraordinary. Something which Jen had kept from Billy since the moment they had met. Jen had lived in fear of this moment for most of her life, but now she had to confront it with the person she loved more than anyone or anything in the world.

Stifling her sobs, Jen spoke.

"I knew you'd find me someday, Billy. Ever since I was six, I knew you'd come looking for me. You see, someone or something, and I'm hoping He's God, also bestowed upon me a gift, or perhaps a curse. When we first met at Madison Square Garden, I had no idea what you'd look like, Billy. I was not given the ability to see the future as you were. I didn't know your name or anything about you. I just knew that you'd come for me eventually."

With that, Jen began sobbing once more and appeared to be disconsolate. As both sat in bed, Billy kissed her and held her before responding.

"It's all right, angel. I'm shaken to the core, but everything will be okay. I love you more than anything in the world, angel."

Billy kissed the tears from Jen's face and swallowed them. Jen attempted to compose herself before replying.

"Billy, I love you with all my heart and soul, but something may not be all right. You see, I knew that if you ever learned the truth about me, that you'd be chosen."

Prophet's End

Billy peered at Jen quizzically before responding. He surmised Jen's inference, itself an improbable, however, accurate conclusion. "I really understand, now, sweetheart. All these years, I believed in my heart that this "gift" was merely an exercise in futility and that it would all be in vain. There just had to be an explanation as to why I was provided these visions."

Billy hesitated briefly before continuing. He was almost hesitant to ask. He gulped before asking.

"Jen, do you know what exactly I was chosen for?"

Jen attempted a tearful smile before responding.

"I'm a devout Christian, as I believe you are, too, Billy. It's in your heart. But I really don't know what you've been chosen for, my love. All I knew is that you'd find me and whatever you were chosen for will be something extreme, something ordained."

Jen made the sign of the cross before continuing.

"Although I'm confident that He will guide you, Billy, I'm a bit frightened."

"Frightened of what, Jen?"

"Frightened that I'll lose you."

"You'll never lose me, Jennifer. Just look in your heart, and I'll always be there."

The former Jennifer Swanson smiled bravely and beckoned for Billy to come to her.

"Hold me, Billy."

With that they embraced. They remained in that embrace until morning.

Chapter Twenty-Five

Do you understand, gentlemen, that in all the horror, there is just this: that there is no horror!

           – Russian Writer Aleksandr Kuprin

Immediately following Billy's admission and Jen's equally stunning confession, all of Billy's dreams vanished; all that is, except one recurring dream. Despite the fact that Billy had been retired from the FDNY for quite some time, he would endure an intermittent dream in which he entered a large burning building, one filled with smoke so thick that he could hardly see for more than a distance of a few feet. In the recurrent dream, Billy would awake with the feeling that he was desperately searching for specific people, but when he awoke, he could not remember who.

Peter, Billy and Jen's son, was now thirty-two years old and a Federal Agent, a U.S. Marshal. Angela, thirty, who had graduated from Princeton University, was a college professor at her alma mater. Billy, fifty-six, remained fit as did Jen, his still unworldly beautiful and inspirational wife. The twenty-first century had commenced and the world continued to change drastically, and not always for the better. It appeared as if many on the planet had lost their respective souls.

On a bright, sunny September day, Billy awoke, kissed Jen tenderly and prepared to leave for lower Manhattan. He was to attend a meeting of retired Police officers and firefighters. Jen held him particularly tight as they embraced. Jen's grip was tighter than ever before, it was as if she did not want to let go.

On that sunlit morning, Billy arrived at the ballroom where the retired Police and Firefighters had congregated. However, his visit was curtailed when alarms rang out signifying that a major incident had taken place, one that required as much help from Police, Fire-fighters and emergency EMTs, active or not. Billy, as did many others in attendance, rushed to the scene of the catastrophe. There were already dozens of responders already battling the blaze and all arrivals were given instructions to proceed past the checkpoint at their own peril. Help was desperately needed, but it was made clear that this was a desperate and dangerous situation.

Sirens sounded, and as people ran or were assisted out of the building, only Police, Firefighters and all First Responders ran towards it. Many of the people exiting from the smoky fiery haze had the look of zombies, their eyes vacuous and fearful. They appeared to be in shock, and the look of disbelief and horror was etched on their faces, and they were the lucky ones. As the smoke grew thicker, more ambulances arrived. Many of the people being carried out of the building were on stretchers, and many of them appeared to be lifeless. There just weren't enough emergency personnel on hand to treat them; more EMTs rushed to the scene, brave young men and women not giving thought to the perils of their occupation. There were lives to save.

Billy was one of the First Responders, retirement be damned. Billy rushed into the building as others ran out, folks covered in soot and ash, men and women wanting desperately to return home to their families and loved ones, men and women whose lives would never be the same.

As soon as Billy entered the burning building, the toxic smoke and dirt seared his lungs. Billy, of course, a veteran of many conflagrations, had never experienced any as devastating. The heat he felt was as intense as any he had endured, his eyes seared with unimaginable soreness as he barged into the deadly fray. Firefighters already in the building were shouting that the elevators were not functioning and that a stairwell evacuation was taking place. It was the only way in which to save what was left of the inhabitants of the building which was now engulfed in flames.

As Billy began to climb the stairs in hopes of rescuing those still alive, there were dead bodies strewn throughout the building, incredibly he began to have a distinct and vivid vision. He recalled wondering for much of his life why he had been chosen to see things, events of the future. Suddenly, he instinctively knew that this was his moment. He had been selected to be at this precise location on this fateful day. He recalled beautiful Jen's words, "Whatever you've been chosen for will be something extreme, something ordained."

It was at that exact moment that Billy began experiencing a vivid Epiphany. It was clear as day, his dreams and visions were now entering his mind fast and furiously. He **KNEW** where to look in order to be the savior for whom he was designated.

"Quick," he thought, "behind the third-floor staircase."

She was there, just as Billy's vision had guided him. But there was a reason! Billy knew it wasn't the Haitian woman he was saving. It was her unborn granddaughter, a woman who would not be born for forty years, a woman who would go on to cure Alzheimer's and Dementia.

The woman choked as Billy carried her down the staircase and out into the street. As he handed her to the EMTs, she called out softly to him, "God bless you!"

But Billy was not done. His visions were coming rapidly. The vision directed him to a fourth-floor office in order to save a young Jamaican man named Desmond. Billy **KNEW** that he'd be trapped beneath a massive file cabinet, gasping for air. As Billy attempted to rescue the entrapped man from below the metal storage case, huge burning debris fell from above, just inches from where he struggled to free the victim. Summoning strength he never even imagined he had, Billy somehow extricated the helpless man from the rubble. The heroic act was witnessed by two other firefighters who watched in amazement and awe at both Billy's improbable strength and bravery. One of the firefighters remarked to the other, "How the hell did he do that?! It's as if he's possessed by the devil!" The other firefighter responded, "If he's possessed, it's by the man upstairs, not the devil!" Billy knew that it was not only the Jamaican man he was saving, but his unborn son, a man who would become a renowned cardiologist.

Billy once more raced into the burning building and ran up the stairs to the fifth floor. Many other firefighters were receiving oxygen in front of the building which had become an inferno, but Billy knew why he had to rush back in. Billy **KNEW** that the man whose life he was saving would have a son who would go on to win a Nobel Peace prize in Medicine. Billy, choking, reached the man at exactly the spot he saw in his vision. However, he knew that his job had not yet ended.

Billy rushed in and raced to the second floor. The young Russian Jewish woman was literally lying face down on the ground. She was rapidly losing consciousness and Billy **KNEW** exactly where he'd find her. He also **KNEW** she would have a grandson who would go on to save dozens of her patients suffering from chronic illnesses as a physician at New York's Sloan Kettering Cancer Institute. Billy gathered her up and raced down the staircase, carrying her to salvation.

Billy was not done, however. He **KNEW** where to find a Rabbi who was visiting a friend on the sixth floor of the building, a young Rabbi who would go on to tutor several youngsters in Israel, many of whom would make significant contributions to society.

Billy was on a mission. Time and time again, he would brave the odds and rescue folks, all with families to go home to, all with promising futures. There were teachers, attorneys, mechanics, librarians and on and on. Billy would literally SEE their families as they returned home to their loved ones, and see them as they entered the homes of those waiting anxiously to see if their husbands, wives, brothers and sisters had survived, and Billy would see them BEFORE he rescued each individual.

Billy rushed back in to save an Islamic woman, a woman in her twenties, a woman whose unborn daughter would go on to become a renowned heart surgeon and save countless lives. He **KNEW** where

75

to find her. She was in the kitchen in her second floor office, hiding behind a closed door, fearful to move. Billy found her at precise the location his vision guided him to. He carried her in his arms out into the street where he handed her to the EMTs.

The EMTs attempted to convince Billy not to reenter the building, which seemed to be engulfed in flames. They sensed accurately that Billy was in dire straits and he too required serious medical attention. However, their efforts to restrain him failed, and Billy rushed back into the inferno. He **KNEW** that he must race back to the fifth floor where he was certain he would find a young pregnant woman who would later give birth to a son, a scientist who would go on to cure Crohn's and Colitis, two previously incurable, insidious diseases. Billy located her where he had envisioned as she lay under a desk, gasping and choking for breath. Billy scooped her up and with all the strength he had left in his failing body, he ran down the treacherous stairs, through a thickening cloud of smoke and onto the street. The young woman was then taken by the EMTS and moments later Billy crumpled to the pavement. He had fulfilled his purpose.

Minutes later, there was a huge booming sound. The building had begun to collapse.

As Billy breathed his last, thoughts feverishly entered his mind. He actually managed a smile as he envisioned Sandy Amoros racing into the left field corner to make a miraculous catch in the 1955 World Series. He dreamed he was sixteen years old and standing in his hero Pete Hamill's doorway at the old *New York Post*, mesmerized at seeing his hero seated at a desk. He dreamed of the absurdity of D.B. Cooper's plane hijacking. And then he dreamed of seeing the visage of a beautiful little six-year-old girl, wonderful Jen. And then he drifted off into his final sleep... It was 9/11.

Postscript

In the year 2017 I wrote "PROPHET'S END" as a tribute to First Responders, my idol Pete Hamill and to beautiful and courageous Jen Bricker, who these days is Jen Bricker-Bauer and she and her wonderful husband Dominik, an Austrian are the proud parents of Malachi their young son!

Obviously being a native New Yorker I was and am deeply affected by the events of 9/11 and the foreign attacks on the United States of America.

A young man named Righteous Osa-Ogbontaen knocked on our door in 2017 and what he told me that afternoon will resonate for the rest of my days here on planet Earth and beyond.

Holding my book aloft for me to see, Righteous smiled and asked, "Do you know who you are? Do you know what you've written?"

I laughed and replied that I indeed often had conflicting thoughts regarding my identity.

Righteous then spoke, "Scott, what you've written is an addendum to the Scriptures!"

Seriously, how does one respond to that?!

The following is what I wrote following Righteous' visit.

Oh, and get this - Righteous is now an ORDAINED MINISTER as is Jen Bricker's wonderful husband, Dominik Bauer and they are now great friends.

I am the one who introduced them!

A RIGHTEOUS VISITOR FROM AFRICA

A SENSE OF FULFILLMENT
REVISITING THE FUTURE

A Righteous Visitor from Africa
A Sense of Fulfillment - Revisiting the Future

Righteous knocked on our door yesterday afternoon. Righteous, and that is his birth name, carried an envelope with him, and in the envelope was a book that I had written nearly anonymously in 2017. The book, *Prophet's End*, was virtually ignored by the masses, something I truthfully anticipated. I am not a renowned author.

Righteous has the black skin of an Ethiopian prince. He is a young, tall, athletic and handsome young man. His eyes seemed to sparkle. He removed the book from the envelope, smiled and said,

"You wrote this. It is a wonderful book. I cried and laughed as I read it. It is the only book I've ever read in one sitting, and I've read many books."

I thanked Righteous and Peggy and I invited him into our home and he graciously accepted the invite.

I would soon learn that his late father was a Holy Man in the African continent, the place that Righteous was born. I thanked him and told him that his reaction upon reading "Prophet's End" was exactly the one I had hoped a reader would experience.

I then told Righteous that First Responders, a young woman named Jennifer Bricker and my idol Pete Hamill had inspired the book.

Once more, Righteous smiled and responded, "You have no idea who you are, do you?" I admitted that I have often struggled with identity, Righteous then offered, "Well, He knows who you are. At the end of the book, you wrote about fulfilling one's purpose. You, also are fulfilling your purpose."

I immediately joked, "I guess that's it, Peggy. This must be the end!"

Righteous laughed and replied, "No, there is much more to be done. You are far from done. This book, your story, must be heard. I'll see to it that it is."

Righteous has seen the future. "Soon, he said, it will be revealed as to who you really are."

Righteous arose from our sofa and said softly, "I have a few more visits to make today, but none will be as extraordinary as this one." Righteous told me that we would meet again.

I anxiously await his reappearance.

NOTE: Righteous indeed reappeared.

He is currently spreading His word in Texas.

Righteous Osa-Agbontaen, Jen Bricker-Bauer, and Peggy Russell

FLESH AND BLOOD
PRELUDE TO PETE

Flesh and Blood
Prelude to Pete

It was a day of overwhelming loss and yet of hope and faith. On Friday morning, he had awoken to the dreary sound of windswept rain cascading down from the drainpipes outside his home. He knew in his heart that this would preclude a trip some two hundred miles away in order to pay final respects to a beloved family member, albeit one who had chosen to no longer communicate. Even family members have been swept away into this frightening age of partisanship. The deceased could no longer tolerate any opinions other than his own. It is the way of the world of 2018.

It is obscene that anyone should pass so tragically and unexpectedly at his tender age, and it bothered him deeply that that the young man had never reached out to perhaps consider a reconciliation. Perhaps, he thought, that he should have tried a little harder, too, although he's always had difficulty in dealing with the atheistic mindset. There was time, he thought, but time, as he's learned, is so precious.

So, he paid his respects from afar and he and his bride of thirty-four years (forty years now) decided that on the following day, yesterday, to make a brief trip in order to join a horde of half-crazed Red Sox celebrants who gathered to meet several of their heroes who were contracted to appear at an annual sports memorabilia show.

The trip was made in a steady drizzle which in no way dismayed the huge throng of Red Sox faithful, who longed to see their conquering heroes. However, he was not there to meet the recently crowned World Series champions, but to meet an incredibly great actor.

As he entered the huge auditorium, he made sure to personally thank as many members of the Aleppo Shriners, those wonderful people who run the Shriner's Hospitals and who have done so much of His remarkable work on the planet Earth. Ask beautiful Jen Bricker about the Shriner's Hospitals and what they have meant to her and countless other children.

Speaking of beautiful Jen Bricker, it was time to educate this remarkable actor about the inspirational, courageous and beautiful young woman. So, he approached "Lewis Gates" and handed the actor an envelope containing a novel titled "Prophet's End" and an unpublished novel/screenplay title "The Scorekeeper," both inspired by Ms. Bricker.

He did not call the actor by his given name, but by a name created by his idol, the incomparable Pete Hamill. He handed him a book to personalize. The actor peered at the book and exclaimed, "Incredibly, I was just thinking about this movie just yesterday!" Rather than his actual name, the actor inscribed the book, "God bless, Irish Bobby Fallon." Often things are not by chance.

Moments earlier, upon entering the auditorium, he had run into a friend he had not seen in quite some time, in fact, several years. The friend, a young man named John Ryan, informed him that he had just been thinking about him and his wife just the other day. John Ryan, then remarked, "You know, of course, that these things are pre-ordained…."

He reached into the bag he was carrying and handed John Ryan a personalized copy of *Prophet's End* and replied, "I know. Please read the book…."

"Gladly," he responded. It's great to see you both!"

As they walked out of the Shriner's Auditorium and towards their car which was parked on a grass lot that had been soaked in several inches of rain upon their arrival, the skies had begun to clear, the winds increased and the sun began to peek out from behind the clouds.

He thought about Him, and hope and faith.

Flesh and Blood

Note: The actor's name is Tom Berenger (Major League), incidentally and he is a GREAT guy!

FINDING MARY

Prologue

Perhaps a few of you might recall my post of October 1, 2017—Mary is still fighting the battle against an insidious disease, but the pretty young woman is a true warrior. I especially worry about her during this humanitarian crisis, since she is much more susceptible.

Oh, and since that glorious day our lives intersected with Mary, and that's her real name, I've actually met my idol, Pete Hamill, too! I don't believe in coincidence.

Finding Mary

The day began ominously enough with a raw wind blowing in menacing clouds above the autumnal New England countryside . He turned his collar up against the chill. The bleak landscape cast a pall over his already somber mood. He and his bride of 33 (40 years now) years arrived at a diner in Plainville, Massachusetts.

As they sat and sipped their coffee, he began ruminating the immediate future. He recently had written a novel entitled "Prophet's End" and was becoming increasingly frustrated in regard to reaching his intended audience. How ironic, he thought, that a story about hope and faith would provide so little hope and faith for the author.

It is a widely accepted fact that the vast majority of writers have one person in mind when creating a composition, lengthy or otherwise. In his case, Prophet's End was an homage to his idol as a youth, the incomparable author, columnist and journalist, Pete Hamill. Hamill, who apparently has experienced some health issues in the recent past, has seemingly vanished from the public eye.

It's as if there is a protective cocoon meticulously constructed around the icon, and that no outsider, especially some unheralded insignificant author is permitted to penetrate that barrier.

As he pondered the increasing possibility that his idol would never learn of the work intended for his eyes, he became disheartened, he felt as if the story he had written was his legacy, perhaps a rite of passage to whatever awaited him on the other side of this life. Of course, he also considered that perhaps Mr. Hamill was doing poorly health wise, and that made him even more doleful.

Later in the day, the threatening skies of the morning opened up and gave way to cold afternoon showers as he and his wife drove south to Providence in order to see a performance of Les Miserables at the Providence Performing Arts Center. The incredibly great work of art was, he thought, anathema for his already semi-depressed state. He managed a laugh as he considered that these already intolerant times may very well be abetted by additional gloominess.

After parking in a lot approximately three blocks from the theater, he and his wife trudged through the rain towards their destination. Around the corner from Weybosset Street where the theater is located, they witnessed a large menacing glowering man spewing angry words at a parking lot attendant. He appeared to be one of a growing army of disenfranchised people roaming the streets of our cities. His eyes were vacant and he appeared to be close to violence.

He quickly guided his wife, Peggy, past the angry human and turned the corner onto Weybosset Street where he knew he'd find a police officer. The African American police officer, an impressive 6' 5" gentleman, immediately sprung into action, quickly calling for backup as he walked briskly towards the incident. The man and his wife continued their trek to the theater, they knew the situation was in good hands.

Upon being seated inside the old elegant theater, they began reading their Playbills. Within minutes two young attractive women took seats directly in front of them. The lovely young woman on the aisle was wheeling in a tank of oxygen and she had tubes in her nose which were attached to the tank. She seemed far too young to have such an apparatus.

With the show still approximately fifteen minutes from beginning, the woman stood up in order to allow someone else to be able to take a seat in her row. At one point in his life, he'd be hesitant to initiate a conversation with a complete stranger, however, he felt compelled to. He himself, had contracted an incurable, insidious and anti immune disease, albeit one that is in current remission. He noted that the young woman winced as she repositioned the tank of oxygen.

He asked, "That looks a bit heavy." The pretty young woman replied, "It is heavy."

Finding Mary

From the expression on her face, he ascertained that she did not particularly mind the intrusion by the older stranger.

"Enjoy the show," he offered.

She smiled sweetly and responded, "It's on my bucket list. My friend here (she patted the other young woman on the head) was wonderful enough to invite me."

She then hugged her friend.

The young woman then continued, "I have MD and my body has begun to shut down. I have always wanted to see this show. I don't know how much longer I have." She laughed and then said, "This theater is wonderful."

The young woman amazed me. He thought that he'd never seen anyone enjoy any event as much as this young lady. At the show's conclusion, after the audience stood and applauded at the amazing performances, she stood and cheered. She then turned and hugged her friend sweetly. There were tears in both their eyes. They then both pivoted quickly and headed towards the lobby before anyone else could vacate their seats.

He suddenly grabbed his wife by the hand. By that time the crowd exiting the theater had grown thick as he rushed through a maze of patrons. He HAD to speak to the young woman. After pushing through a sea of humanity, he reached her just before she had made it to the doors to the street.

"Young lady, " he spoke. "I must tell you that you are truly incredible. Your spirit and courage is palpable."

The young woman, already in tears, burst out sobbing. implausibly, she apologized!

"I'm so sorry," she spoke, "I can't help myself."

He replied, "There is nothing to apologize for. You are beyond wonderful!"

She responded, "You are wonderful!"

The young woman reached out and hugged the older man.

The older man and the younger woman exchanged contact information.

As the older man exited into the street, he saw the police officer who had responded to his earlier request. He smiled at the older man and said, "We took care of the situation. We took him to the hospital. Hopefully, he can get some help." He looked up into the sky. The clouds were gone and replaced with bright sunshine.

Just this morning, the man was feeling forlorn about not finding his idol, Pete Hamill, but in the process he found Mary. All in all it was a good day.

Mary Sarkees is her name, incidentally.

She is still, thank God, fighting her courageous battle.

Oh, and I indeed got to meet Mr. Hamill.

My hero did NOT disappoint me.

My scribblings from December 12, 2018

Note: My idol, Pete Hamill passed on August 5, 2020, over four years ago:

LIFE AND OTHER ANTIQUITIES

LIFE AND OTHER ANTIQUITIES

There was a time in the irretrievable past that some people engaged in civil discourse and overwhelming intolerance was not the norm.

Implausibly as it may seem, there existed intelligent conservative Republicans such as #42, the great Jackie Robinson and William F. Buckley.

This was a glorious time before right-wing "liberals" spewed their invective, a time before an inarticulate cretin of a president, a former Democrat (#45) so unnerved them that they were moved to unintentionally prove what the legendary Mort Sahl ATTEMPTED to teach us, that the far left and far right were one and the same.

During this glorious bygone period, great journalists roamed the streets of our cities, none greater though, than my idol, the incomparable Pete Hamill.

Pete Hamill, the son of immigrants who hailed from Belfast in Northern Ireland, graced the pages of the New York Post, the New York Daily News, the Village Voice and numerous other journals.

There existed no subtlety in Hamill's writings, just a powerful Mike Tyson or an "Irish Bobby Fallon" like punch in the mouth.

Each morning or late afternoon (there were morning and evening editions of most major dailies) as I rode the IRT to Manhattan to or from my places of gainful employment, I would stop at a newsstand with the hope that Pete Hamill had perhaps experienced a bad cup of coffee or been witness to some form of iniquity.

I was never disappointed upon reading Hamill's chronicles, all of which were written with a passion and brutal honesty I had never before seen.

As the son of Billy Hamill and the former Annie Devlin, Pete was raised with compassion for the poor, the oppressed, the disadvantaged and the downtrodden. His sensitivity to injustice was palpable and manifested through his powerful words.

Two evenings ago (Monday, Dec. 10, 2018), thanks to a lovely young woman named Miriam Nyhan-Grey, the Associate Director of Glucksman Ireland House of NYU, I was privileged to meet my idol, the one and only Pete Hamill. I was hesitant, for many years I had invariably left my heroes at a distance, however, Ms. Grey insisted that I do so.

"Nonsense," she exclaimed in her wonderful Irish brogue, "you traveled a long distance to meet Peter."

Peggy, my long suffering bride of 34 years (40 years now) and I invited two guests to "A Tribute to Pete Hamill" at NYU's Rosenthal Pavilion, our dearest friends, Dr. Vladimir Privman, a brilliant endocrinologist at New York's Lutheran Hospital, and his lovely wife, Dr. Violetta Thierbach, both immigrants much like Pete Hamill's brave parents who had emigrated here to find a better life.

As Peggy and I entered the auditorium in which the tribute was to take place, I peered around the room and noted that the vast majority of the crowd were our contemporaries. That is, they all appeared to be senior citizens, all seemingly from a nearly extinct era, all harking back to the days during which New Yorkers were privileged to read the prose of Jimmy Breslin, Jimmy Cannon and yes, Pete Hamill.

The dais resembled an all-star team of legendary journalists. One by one, they each paid homage to Pete Hamill with remembrances that were both hilarious and poignant. On several occasions I had to wipe the tears that were welling in my eyes. The presenters were each extraordinary writers.

Ms. Miriam Nyhan-Grey read tributes from Gloria Steinem and the Babe Ruth of salsa, the magnificent Ruben Blades, the genius singer, songwriter, actor and activist from Panama.

Life and Other Antiquities

There was Dan Barry, James McBride, Mike Lupica, Joanna Molloy, Jim Dwyer, Mike Barnicle, Sam Roberts, Peggy Noonan, Carl Hiassen, Charles Sennott, and of course, Denis Hamill, the younger brother of Pete, who himself is an outstanding novelist in his own right.

Seriously, I did not belong there, but I had been invited.

The legendary folk singer Judy Collins concluded the proceedings with a rousing rendition of "Amazing Grace," and we all joined in.

There were numerous other renowned writers in the audience.

There won't be any more Pete Hamills, of this I'm certain. We've gone from Frank Sinatra to Kanye, from Stravinsky to Tiny Tim, from the Drifters to Justin Bieber, from Sidney Poitier to Charlie Sheen, from Audrey Hepburn to Lindsay Lohan. Mozart has indeed, gone blind and most youngsters could not tell you who Pete Hamill is, or who Mike Royko was, but they know the names of hip hop artists who objectify and denigrate women, and if a motion picture does not include sorcerers, dinosaurs or vampires, well, no thanks.

As I prepared to leave without meeting my idol (leave your idols at a distance) Mr. Hamill, I thanked Ms. Miriam Nyhan-Gray for inviting me to this remarkable event.

Ms. Nyhan-Gray had previously presented a copy of my work, "Prophet's End" to Mr. Hamill, and I wasn't about to ask if he had read it.

With a multitude of magnificent legendary journalists present, I felt like a fish out of water. I was a Little Leaguer hanging with Willie Mays and Sandy Koufax.

Upon thanking Ms. Nyhan-Gray and introducing myself to her, Ms. Nyhan-Gray inquired "And whom might you be?"

Upon identifying myself, Ms. Nyhan-Gray addressed me as follows:

"Nonsense," Miriam Nyhan-Grey exclaimed with her lilting Irish brogue. "You traveled a long distance to meet Peter, and you will meet your hero!"

The great Pete Hamill, who in recent years has endured heart problems (he is now deceased), type-two diabetes and suffered a fall in which he broke both hips simultaneously, peered deeply into my eyes and grasped my hand firmly and spoke.

"Thank you," he said, "Thank you."

Four words!

During our trip back to Vladimir and Violetta's home in Brooklyn, birthplace of my idol, Pete Hamill, I was strangely silent. Those that know me are aware of that being an extremely remote possibility.

Finally, Dr. Vladimir Privman broke the silence.

"So, Scott, are you ever going to wash your hand again?"

PART II

COVIDIAN SUMMER

WHAT LIES BENEATH

What Lies Beneath

Chapter One

Mark Bradford was having a few drinks with some of his old law school friends at the "Top of the Hub" in Boston's Prudential Center when Palmer Stevenson appeared at the door with her friend, Marisa Delgado. Upon seeing Palmer's stunningly attractive face and checking out her long shapely legs and shapely body, Mark dropped the fork he had been holding in his right hand.

"Damn," he said, "I'm in lust!" Mark began to excuse himself from the table at which his associates, Bobby Levane and Max Cannizaro sat and muttered, "I'll be right back, guys. I've got to meet this chick,"

After a short and somewhat banal conversation with his intended target, Mark returned somberly to his table.

"I think I just got shot down, but man, what a doll and did you see her rack? I gave her my card. She's a veterinarian. I think I'll bring my cat to her office for a checkup."

Bobby Levane responded, "Hey, Mark, you don't even have a cat!"

"Hey, I'll borrow your cat, Max. Isn't she due for a checkup?"

Max answered nervously, "Are you kidding me? Do you really think you've got a chance with this girl? Besides, you and Chrissy have been together for what, two years? Are you trying to break Chrissy's heart? Last week you were considering popping the question."

Mark would soon follow through with his plan. He even borrowed his sister's cat.

"Where there's a piece like that," Mark spewed, "there's a way."

Chapter Two

The conflagration could be seen for miles. The billowing smoke and the flashing of red lights from emergency vehicles approaching the scene of which was assuredly an awful accident, served as a traffic advisory for the now stopped traffic on I-495 going in both directions. The date was late Saturday evening July 7, 2018, and Palmer Annabelle Stevenson's entire life had forever changed.

To this moment, Palmer does not retain a single memory of the horrific crash that nearly took her then twenty-two-year-old life. Palmer had just celebrated with some of her closest friends at her engagement party which took place at Abigail Farms Restaurant in Methuen, Massachusetts and she was being driven home by her dearest friend and confidante, Eleanor Jameson, who already had been chosen to be her bridesmaid at Palmer's forthcoming wedding in October. Neither of the young women saw the tractor trailer that had spun out of control and crossed the median strip, but they certainly felt its devastating impact.

In Eleanor's case, thanks to the grace of God or perhaps pure luck, although she was thrown from the vehicle, she escaped with minor injuries, which albeit included a broken left arm. Palmer, however, was not as fortunate. Palmer had been knocked senseless, but even more awful was the result of the windshield shattering which left countless shards of glass imbedded deeply into her face, but then even a worse unimaginable scenario occurred. The vehicle burst into flames with Palmer strapped firmly beneath her seatbelt and rendered completely unconscious.

As those in the four-mile long backup on the interstate peered ahead to the fiery and frightening scene unfolding, most sat in shocked silence, dismayed not by the delay in reaching their destinations, but what they considered to be a major catastrophic and likely fatal situation. By the time the paramedics arrived at the grisly scene, there was little hope that Palmer would survive the disaster.

As the firefighters and ambulance personnel worked feverishly to extinguish the fire and extricate what was left of Palmer Stevenson from the smoldering vehicle, some first responders seemed overcome with emotion, although as is invariably the case, their actions certainly saved Palmer's life, at least temporarily.

With Palmer's facial skin having been charred to a crisp, she was immediately hooked to an oxygen tank and upon arrival at Holy Family Hospital in Methuen, she was placed into a medically induced coma. The lone positive news was that the fire had not reached her eyes or lips. It was at Holy Family that Palmer remained in a coma for seven days.

Chapter Three

Palmer Stevenson is one of the most beautiful women on the planet. At least she was considered that by most until the horrific events of July 7, 2018. Initially, Palmer was not allowed any visitors during the time she was in ICU, although her dearest friend, Eleanor Jameson, the driver of the ill-fated vehicle, remained in the hospital for the entire evening following the tragic car crash. However, Eleanor was not present due to her injuries, which were not life-threatening, but because she refused to leave Palmer's side, despite Palmer not being aware of her, or anyone else's presence.

Eleanor slept in a makeshift bed provided to her by hospital employees. Upon being made aware of the horrifying accident, Palmer's fiancé Mark Bradford rushed feverishly to Holy Family Hospital, but was immediately informed that it would not be possible for him to see or visit his betrothed. Mark, an aspiring attorney, was informed that Palmer was in ICU with life-threatening injuries including head trauma, severe burns and that she was hooked up to a ventilator. After hugging Eleanor, who had firmly insisted she maintain a vigil at the hospital, Mark left, and before the evening was done, he had joined some friends at a bar back home in Boston, in order to drown his sorrows. Mark would not return to the hospital until he would be permitted to physically see Palmer.

The following day, Palmer's doctors and her mom and dad, Albert and Marie Stevenson, convinced Eleanor to return home to Brookline, Massachusetts. Palmer remained in ICU, but her condition although still critical, was upgraded to stable. Palmer's face was covered with bandages and ice was constantly supplied. The doctors at Holy Family Hospital were aware that such a burn patient should be relocated to Massachusetts General Hospital in Boston, that is, as soon as she regained consciousness and was considered well enough to be transported.

What Lies Beneath

On July 15, 2018, Palmer finally regained semi-consciousness. She had been administered morphine and other formidable drugs for her to tolerate the enormous pain she was enduring, but her awareness due to both the meds and her condition, made it nearly impossible for her to communicate. With her family and friends at her side, including Eleanor, Palmer's fiancé, Mark hurriedly arrived at the hospital upon learning that Palmer had awakened.

As Mark sat at her bedside, nurses arrived to change the dressing on the bandages covering Palmer's face. Upon seeing the bandages lifted, Mark winced as for the initial time, he saw the calamitous results of his fiancée's charred face. Mark, who had been holding Palmer's hand up until that point, immediately excused himself, left the room and staggered down to a restroom where he proceeded to throw up. Overwhelmed, without telling anyone, Mark left the hospital and drove home to Boston.

Chapter Four

Upcoming graduating from Brookline High School, Palmer Stevenson studied veterinary medicine at Cornell University. Lovely shapely and ebullient, Palmer's friends attempted to convince her to campaign for "homecoming queen," and although she refused, they entered her into the competition and she won, to no one's surprise, but to her consternation. Palmer never once flaunted her immense beauty or extraordinary gifts. There was nothing superficial about Palmer.

Palmer, who unabashedly loved animals, started her own veterinary practice in Newton, Massachusetts upon receiving her degree from the prestigious Ivy League college. Within months, Palmer added Dr. Vanessa Trembley to her veterinarian staff. Vanessa, an old and dear friend of Palmer's mom, had been a respected vet for several years. The two women made for a great team.

Palmer never dressed sensationally or wore much makeup, her natural looks never requiring enhancement. She was not merely attractive but was once described as a "pulverizing beauty." But it was her effervescence and her zest for life that set her apart, her singular spirit and overt friendliness and compassion coming naturally. That and her unabashed love for animals.

Palmer had met Mark, her fiancé, at a Boston's "Top of the Hub," where Mark began successfully mesmerizing her with his sharp wit and acerbic tongue. Although she thought him to be a bit of a blowhard, she was impressed with his intelligence, his enterprise, and his commitment to become an attorney. Mark had graduated near the top of his class at Suffolk Law. Palmer was physically attracted to Mark, but more so to his energy. In Mark's case, however, he had fallen in love, or to be more accurate, in lust with Palmer at first sight.

Upon returning to Boston after having regurgitated at the sight of Palmer's unbandaged face at Holy Family Hospital, Mark joined several of his acquaintances at a local watering hole. After a few drinks, a visibly shaken and more than slightly inebriated Mark spewed, "I'm not sure if I can handle it. Palmer's a mess. I don't know if she'll ever look good again."

After ten days at Holy Family Hospital, it was decided by the attending physicians including two prominent Massachusetts Hospital surgeons, to make plans to airlift Palmer to the MGH Burn facility in downtown Boston. Months of painful skin grafts were soon scheduled, and countless hours of surgeries planned for the beautiful veterinarian. However, it would be months before any such endeavor would take place. There was healing to do, and reconstruction of that nature requires enormous preparation and precise strategy.

Upon Palmer's relocation to Massachusetts General Hospital, Mark would visit, but his visits grew increasingly shorter and often there were days at a time when he would inform Palmer that he had to work late and couldn't visit that particular day. On those occasions that nurses and technicians would enter Palmer's room to change her dressing, he would immediately leave the area before the bandages were removed.

Palmer had never seen how she herself appeared, as she religiously avoided mirrors, being truly fearful as to how she would view herself. However, it was obvious upon seeing Mark's reaction as to how horrific she appeared to him. At no time was their upcoming wedding discussed, at least with Mark, but Palmer's parents informed their daughter that the plans including the wedding and reception, had been "postponed" to a later unspecified date, and for Palmer to not concern herself with anything other than healing. Then one day, Palmer walked from her hospital bed to the mirror in the bathroom after her bandages had been removed and not yet replaced with new gauze and covering. Palmer gasped. Although beautiful Palmer Stevenson never took her natural beauty seriously, she was entirely shocked at what she considered to be the hideous reflection peering back at her in the mirror.

Devastated at seeing for the initial time what she now looked like, Palmer began trembling uncontrollably and sobbing. After attempting to compose herself, she returned to her room where the nurses were waiting to change her dressing and bandages. The older nurse, Sylvia, then spoke:

"Palmer, you'll be amazed at what they can accomplish with plastic surgery these days. These doctors are incredible."

Not thinking of herself, Palmer thought, "Poor Mark. I can't even imagine what he's thinking."

Chapter Five

Mark had finished his workday and repaired to a bar on Harvard Street in Brookline. After downing his third beer, Mark turned to his two colleagues, Ralph and James and blurted out, "I don't know how much longer I can do this, guys. Palmer's face is really messed up. Shit, to be truthful, she's sort of grotesque."

Ralph and James, two aspiring attorneys were more than slightly taken aback by Mark's sudden admission. After all, they had often spent time with the couple socially and had little or no knowledge of how to respond to the surprising revelation. James, after briefly hesitating, offered, "Well, I'm sure with the healing process, plastic surgery and time, Palmer's looks will improve commensurately."

Upon Palmer's release from the hospital, she would return for weekly visits to see her surgeons and to undergo additional skin grafts, and plans were being formulated for the young veterinarian to schedule a series of major operations, ones in which an actual new face would be created. On one of these visits, Palmer and her parents found themselves walking down Cambridge Street in Boston, and Palmer's bandages had been temporarily removed in order for her to facilitate quicker healing by exposing her partially repaired face to normal atmospheric conditions. It was then that they walked past a young mother with her six- year-old daughter in tow. Upon seeing Palmer's severely burned face, the child suddenly pointed to Palmer and shouted, "Look, Mommy! Look at her!"

The youngster's mother was completely humiliated and scolded her daughter, "It's not polite to point at people!"

Palmer reacted by laughing hysterically, but inside, her emotions were churning. Palmer told the embarrassed mother, "It's all right. It's perfectly normal for her to react that way. I was in a serious accident."

The woman grabbed her daughter by the hand and led her away while softly answering, "I'm so sorry. I apologize. God bless you." As soon as the mother and child were no longer in range, Palmer once more laughed nervously and told her parents, "She appeared as horrified as Mark!"

Albert and Marie Stevenson were surprised, albeit a bit relieved at hearing their daughter's observation regarding her fiancé, Mark. They had both witnessed Mark's reactions as he flinched each time her bandages were removed, but this was the woman he was betrothed to marry. Unlike the child who pointed and exclaimed her shock, most adults were conditioned to not stare at people with deformities, but the expression on Mark's face was one of revulsion. Palmer's parents had discussed in private, of course, that Mark's less frequent visits to the hospital and his interaction with their daughter had apparently been nothing more than some painful and mandatory task he was obligated to perform.

The following day, Palmer calmingly removed the engagement ring from her finger, and placed it into a velvet jewelry box and handed it to her loving parents, who still adored her as much as the day she was born.

"I believe you know what to do with this," Palmer said quietly, "it doesn't feel right on my finger." Although tears welled in Palmer's beautiful eyes, her sad smile belied her inner turmoil. A great weight had been lifted.

Chapter Six

Obviously, as all beautiful women do, Palmer Stevenson was aware of how she appeared to most men. However, despite her otherworldly beauty, she never took that facet too seriously. As most attractive women are, she was aware that an alarming percentage of the male species included complete strangers who had nothing better to do with their lives than to leer at her, not to mention the more crude members offering obscene comments as she did nothing more than to exist in their presence.

The accident and the resulting disfiguration incurred, of course, changed Palmer's perspective. No, she did not enjoy wolf-calls and the like from the imbeciles who routinely walk our streets, but she would often think of how they'd react if she suddenly lowered her mask to display her now altered appearance. Her prior modest conservatively attired beauty was seldom enhanced by suggestive clothing, but Palmer's natural shapeliness remained evident to any men, and women for that matter, who would view her as she walked by. At no time, however, did Palmer envision the time when a child would be either shocked or repulsed by her face.

Palmer's popularity among her female friends was further complemented by her humility. She was humble and unpretentious. Suddenly, however, she had been thrust into a world where adults would avert their eyes and children would simply gawk.

Chapter Seven

David Grace became aware of the existence of Dr. Palmer Stevenson because of the illness of his three- year-old Labrador retriever, "Reggie." Approximately three months before Palmer's horrific life-changing accident, Reggie had become listless and refused to eat. His lethargy became increasingly worrisome to Dave and his initial visits to a veterinarian's office provided little if any solution to whatever ailed his beloved dog. Having had rescued Reggie from a pound when he was merely a pup, Dave grew progressively more worried and saddened at seeing his pooch deteriorate.

Laura, Dave's sister met her brother for lunch one day and informed him that a co-worker had told her of a magnificent young veterinarian named Palmer Stevenson who had performed miracles for other affected animals. Since Dave, a popular radio disc jockey was extremely busy with his responsibilities, Laura volunteered to take Reggie to see the "miracle worker," Dr. Palmer Stevenson.

Within days of Reggie's visit to the beautiful vet, the dog began to regain his former vitality. Palmer had discovered a little-known virus and had treated Reggie with an effective antibiotic whose positive impact was nearly immediate. Reggie regained full health and Dave was beyond thrilled he had his close sidekick back. But it was the photograph of Dr. Palmer Stevenson with Reggie that caught Dave's eye. Laura wanted her brother to see the astoundingly stunning young veterinarian with Reggie, so she asked Palmer if she would pose. Palmer, of course, laughed, and promptly acquiesced.

"She's the vet that cured Reggie?! Is she a vet or a friggin' beauty queen?" asked Dave, "How about an introduction?" Laura immediately gave her brother the bad news:

"I'm afraid she's engaged to be married."

"That figures. She saved my dog, the least I could've done was to "thank" her."

Laura laughed and replied, "Yes, I'm quite sure every guy would like to "thank" her."

It wasn't until April of 2020, that Dave Grace would hear Palmer Stevenson's name again. As the deadly COVID19 virus spread like wildfire and brought the entire planet to its knees, Laura and Dave, who was still single, got together at their parents' home in Brookline and Laura asked her brother, "Do you remember the veterinarian, Palmer Stevenson, who saved Reggie?"

"Of course, I do."

"Well, she was in the news recently. She was in a horrible automobile accident. She survived, but she was burned badly, and she's undergone hundreds of hours of plastic surgery to have her face restored."

With that, Lorena showed Dave the Boston Globe article describing Palmer's ordeal. The photographs in the article included "before and after" images of the young veterinarian. The piece also contained various quotes by the doctor and Palmer, who stated jokingly, "I now look like a 'cabbage patch' kid. I scare myself when I look in the mirror. It's a good thing I get to wear a mask with this darned virus. I don't wish to frighten young children."

Dave peered at the side-by-side photos of Palmer Stevenson, and asked, "So, it's still Palmer Stevenson? Did she retain her maiden name when she got married?"

Laura responded, "No, she never got married. Read the rest of the story. Her fiancé couldn't handle the way she now looked."

Dave once more looked at Palmer Stevenson's forever lost portrait and her current "cabbage patch" image. All he saw was what lied beneath. Without informing his sister, Laura, Dave, who initially had a severe but positive chemical reaction nearly two years earlier upon seeing the photograph of Reggie with Dr. Stevenson, decided it was high time he switched veterinarians. Therefore, he made an appointment for Reggie to see his savior. The story of beautiful Palmer's nearly tragic accident, her fight to survive, her spirit and her self-deprecating wit regarding her appearance, and her courage to face the world with a remarkable attitude, made him desire her in more ways imaginable. Of course, he realized that Palmer, at least emotionally, bore scars beneath the surface, ones that made her cry when she was alone. David Grace was correct in that regard. Palmer was indeed much more than physically damaged as her scars were also deeply emotional.

Chapter Eight

It was on Monday, June 15, 2020 that handsome David Grace, the popular Boston D.J. arrived at Palmer Stevenson's Newton office with his now five- year-old dog, Reggie. He had made the appointment over the phone, but the name Dave Grace did not ring a bell with Palmer, nor did "Reggie," since it is a common name for pets. With COVID-19 protocols in place, Dave and Reggie were instructed to wait outside in their automobile until their appointment time occurred, and until Palmer had completely disinfected her entire examination room. However, when they were called in by Aubrey, Palmer's technician, Reggie yelped as he recognized the voice of the doctor who had cured him.

"Is that you, Reggie?" Palmer called out in glee, "Oh my God, you look wonderful!"

Palmer smiled from beneath her mask which covered everything but her astonishingly flashing eyes. Dave, already infatuated with Palmer despite knowing what lied beneath her mask, grinned beneath his mask.

"So, you're the miracle doctor who saved my pooch!" Dave declared. "I still have the photograph my sister, Laura took of you two!"

"Yes, I recall your sister telling me what a wreck you were, but I'm hardly a miracle worker. I just found the proper antibiotic, and it worked. I had success with a German Shepherd with that same antidote prior to treating Reggie."

With that, Dave produced the photo of the pre-accident Palmer and his beloved dog. Palmer winced briefly upon seeing her former self, fully knowing that Dave would most likely be at least a bit put off at her current profile. She also thought to herself, that Dave was extremely attractive, but was grateful that he would not learn of her hidden features.

Reggie underwent a complete physical examination upon which Palmer happily announced that Dave's dog was in outstanding physical condition and congratulated the owner for taking great care of his pet. Dave took a deep breath before asking:

"Dr. Stevenson, I hope I'm not being too forward, and I suspect you're already spoken for, but I'd love to repay you for saving Reggie's life a couple of years ago. I'd be honored if I could take you to dinner and perhaps the theater. I can assure you that my intentions are honorable."

Palmer was taken aback, fully knowing that it was doubtful that Dave would have considered such a proposition if he had known that the photograph of her with his dog would never be replicated.

"Dave, that's awfully sweet, but I'm hesitant during this COVID crisis to venture out to restaurants or theaters."

"So, is that a maybe?"

Palmer laughed and responded, "Maybe."

Dave replied, "I know a couple of places with outside seating who strictly adhere to facial coverings and all other required protocol including disinfectants, social distancing, but I'll have to leave Reggie home."

Palmer, despite her inclination to politely decline the date invitation, was surprised by hearing her own voice answer, "I guess it would be all right."

Dave anxiously jotted down Palmer's telephone number and email address. He was firmly convinced he had met the girl of his dreams. Palmer, full of trepidation, wondered to herself why she agreed to set herself up for additional disappointment and disillusionment.

Chapter Nine

Dave realized he would have to proceed delicately in his pursuit of beautiful Palmer Stevenson. Being fully aware of how horrible she would feel if he removed her mask and exhibited even a hint of revulsion at her countenance, David tread lightly.

Taking her to dinner at a restaurant in Newton, Massachusetts, he made certain to make every effort to not even look at Palmer's mask, but on occasion, he would peer into her extraordinarily beautiful eyes. In truth, he was mesmerized by both her spirit and her doe-eyed beauty but made a concentrated effort at not staring at her face. Palmer, on the other hand, often thought of how disappointed Dave would be if he knew of her disfiguration, especially when considering how he initially viewed her photograph with his dog, Reggie.

The one thing that most captivated Dave regarding Palmer's face were her perfectly shaped beautiful lips. He longed to kiss those lips and tell her that he knew exactly what she looked like and that he didn't care how anyone else perceived her. Dave was clearly in love with Palmer, even if she had described herself to her dearest friend, Eleanor as "Bedtime Bunny Bee," her favorite cabbage patch doll as a child. "If only he knew," thought Palmer.

On that initial date, much was discussed, most of it revolving around Palmer's career as a veterinarian, but eventually the conversation turned to music. It was then that Palmer and Dave really connected, as they both realized they loved '60's folk rock, the Motown sound, Delta blues, Bob Dylan and the Band, but it was when Palmer announced that her favorite band was the Eagles, that Dave was more convinced than ever that Palmer was heaven sent.

"They're my favorite band, too!" Dave exclaimed.

"No way," Palmer responded, "you're just attempted to justify liking me."

"I don't have to 'justify' liking you, Palmer, I'm already crazy about you!"

"What? Just because I found the right antidote for your dog, and because you recalled the photo your sister had of me and Reggie? What if I told you my looks have changed since that photo was taken?"

"It wouldn't matter."

"Sure, it wouldn't!"

"I'm serious," Dave replied, "it really wouldn't."

Palmer was having far too much fun to ruin Dave's evening by removing her mask covering her entire face, but not her mouth and eyes. The mask, in fact, was especially designed for Palmer, considering her disfiguration. As much as she desired to display what was what she considered a horrifying truth, Palmer desperately wanted to see Dave again.

Upon taking Palmer home following dinner, Dave asked if he could kiss her.

"Are you sure?" asked Palmer. "It could open an entirely different can of worms. Something that might shock you."

"Please shock me."

Palmer nearly recoiled as Dave gently placed his hands on her shoulders and kissed her tenderly. He immediately felt light-headed. Palmer felt Dave's kiss deeply. As wonderful as it made her feel, she also felt a doleful sadness, knowing in her heart that her charade would be short-lived. After Dave left, Palmer cried herself to sleep.

Chapter Ten

During Palmer's visit to her parents' home the following afternoon, she confided to her mom:

"I met this really nice guy, Dave. He hasn't seen me with my mask off. I cured his dog of a deadly virus a few years ago. I didn't meet him then, his sister had brought his dog to my office, but he saw a photograph of me and his Labrador we had taken back then. He returned to my office a short while ago and he asked me out. I foolishly agreed to have dinner with him."

"It wasn't a foolish thing to do, dear. If he really likes you, he'll like you the way you are."

"That's the problem, mom. I think he loves me. He has no idea."

"Well, if he's that hung up on your current state of affairs, then it's his loss, sweetheart."

Palmer sighed and responded:

"Mom, the problem is that I think I'm in love with him. He's terrific and we have so much in common. But I think my heart would break if he were repulsed by how I look."

Marie Stevenson had no idea how to reply to her brilliant daughter, knowing fully well that her fear was both logical and cogent. Marie reached out and hugged Palmer and squeezed her tightly.

Palmer had agreed to again have dinner with Dave on a Wednesday evening to "break up the workweek." As they walked down Marlborough Street in Boston's Back Bay, one of those unexpected, but nevertheless harrowing events of a person's lifetime struck Palmer out of the blue. Paige Wilhelmson, an animal control-officer and a former colleague of Palmer's suddenly appeared in front of them as the couple walked towards Boston Common. Paige was aware of

Palmer's terrifying accident but had not seen her since before it occurred. Paige squinted, not being certain of it being Palmer behind the mask.

"Palmer, is that you?"

Palmer was mortified and not in the least prepared for Dave finding out about her disfiguration by a stranger he had never met. Dave, of course, was cognizant of why his girlfriend had suddenly stiffened and let go of his hand. Dave was perhaps as frightened by what he accurately perceived as Palmer's trepidation.

Paige peered intently at Palmer's eyes which appeared as if they had seen a ghost.

"Palmer, it's so great to see you! I heard about your accident. How are you doing?"

"I've recovered nicely." Palmer replied, "How are you, Paige?"

It was Dave who intentionally changed the subject.

"Hi, Paige, I'm David Grace. It's nice to meet you."

Paige smiled and asked, "Dave Grace of WBCN Radio?"

"Guilty," Dave replied, "I hope you tune in."

"I thought I recognized your voice. You folks are fun to listen to."

After Palmer and Paige exchanged additional pleasantries, Dave mentioned that they'd be late for the dinner reservation and apologized to Paige for the abrupt end to the conversation. Palmer was briefly silent until the couple were seated at the downtown eatery.

"Dave, I noticed that you weren't particularly interested when Paige asked about my recovery from an accident. I thought that somewhat peculiar. You are not even aware of my accident, are you?"

"Should I be? Whatever occurred, it certainly has not affected you adversely. Has it?

Palmer's lips curled. She had no idea how to respond, especially while seated in a restaurant, one in which "social distancing" was strictly enforced, but still had a decent crowd seated at tables throughout the dining room. "God," she thought, "I cannot allow this charade to continue much longer. I really like this guy and he seems to adore me."

Palmer made a mental note to speak with her parents to discuss the close call involving Paige and her tenuous future regarding her boyfriend. Once more, she cried herself to sleep.

Chapter Eleven

Dave Grace was perhaps as relieved as Palmer upon seeing that her former colleague, Paige, had changed the subject matter, due in large part to Dave's immediate intervention. However, Dave was still not certain it was perhaps time to apprise Palmer that he was aware of her life-altering mishap. The look of vulnerability he saw in Palmer's eyes tore at his heartstrings. He wanted desperately to tell her that her radical metamorphosis in no way altered her innate beauty in his eyes.

As the critically acclaimed voice of the most popular rock station in New England, Dave's image was well known to many despite the fact he was a radio, and not a television personality. Being tall and handsome and outgoing, Dave was often seen on the tube and was the subject of numerous newspaper and magazine articles. In the past calendar year, Dave was featured in Boston Magazine as "Beantown's Most Eligible Bachelor" and on WCVB's popular nightly "Chronicle." Therefore, when Boston Globe entertainment writer, Courtney Donovan cornered him as he left the studio one evening, she thrust a candid photograph of Dave and Palmer walking hand in hand in Boston's Back Bay in his face and asked, "So, who is this girl? I'd love to get the scoop."

Dave being a media veteran, although startled at seeing the image of himself and Palmer, both of course, wearing masks, he countered with, "I'd really prefer to keep this private, but her name is Rebecca Underwood, she's from Victoria, British Columbia, and she's an aspiring actress."

"Can I print that?"

Dave smiled beneath his mask and responded, "Only if you insist."

Meanwhile, back home, Palmer was in deep conversation with her mom, informing her of her close call with her former colleague, Paige, and how Dave quickly changed the subject, something Marie Stevenson thought odd.

"That does seem unusual, Palmer. You'd think he'd want to know everything about you."

"I know, mom, but he's very different, unlike anyone I've ever met."

"He'll have to learn sooner or later, sweetheart. Just know that no matter what happens, we love you very much."

Palmer and her mom hugged. Palmer did not see the tears welling in her mother's eyes.

Chapter Twelve

At Dave's apartment, Palmer dropped Courtney Donovan's "expose" identifying the identity of his girlfriend onto his chest and coyly asked, "Rebecca Underwood, aspiring actress?"

Dave smiled and winced and then responded:

"I just didn't think it's the public's business to know who my girlfriend is."

Palmer replied, "Or perhaps you don't want them to know?"

"Don't be silly. You should know by now that I adore you."

Dave hesitated before continuing:

"I was thinking it's high time we took this to an entirely higher-level, don't you think?"

Dave's mask was off since they were indoors, but Palmer's, as it invariably did, remained in place.

"David, I may not be who or what you think I am?"

"That's bullshit, and you know it. Listen, Palmer, if you haven't figured it out by now, I'm head over heels and hopelessly in love with you."

Dave arose from his seat on the sofa, took Palmer by the hand and led her to the bedroom. They had never been intimate, but despite Palmer's fears, she allowed it to happen, the mask covering her face remaining intact only exposing her beautiful lips and flashing eyes.

Afterwards, they remained silently in bed for over an hour as Dave held her tenderly. Palmer finally broke the silence:

"Why do you love me, David? Was it my saving your dog, the photograph of me that your sister took afterwards? Why exactly do you love me?"

"It should be obvious why I love you, Palmer. You're the only one I've ever known who knew that the members of the original "Eagles" were Glenn Frey, Don Henley, Bernie Leadon and Randy Meisner!"

"Be serious for a moment!"

"All right, pumpkin. You also knew that Don Felder joined the group in '74 and that Joe Walsh replaced Bernie Leadon in '75."

"Is that all? That's why you love me?!"

Dave sighed and said softly, "You're right. There's more."

"That's better. Now tell me why you REALLY love me."

Dave attempted to look serious, but answered, "You also knew that Randy Meisner left in '77 and was replaced by Timothy B. Schmit."

Palmer stifled a laugh and exclaimed, "You're incorrigible!"

Dave sat up in bed, took a deep breath and spoke:

"Listen, Palmer. There are certain things in life that are unexplainable and the most undefinable of these are chemical reactions. I love you, Palmer. I love you with every fiber of my soul. I do not want to live my life without you. I'm hoping that you feel in some way the same about me."

"I do love you, David. I love you very much…but it's complicated."

"Then we'll work it out. Please don't give up on me, pumpkin."

"I'll try not to."

Dave arose from bed and began putting his clothes on. He stood up as Palmer rested her head against a pillow. Dave suddenly reached into his pants pocket and removed a velvet box. Dropping to a knee, he spoke tenderly:

"Palmer Stevenson. Will you marry me?"

Palmer gasped. She waved her hands furiously in front of her covered face. Her insides were churning. She desperately wanted to respond, "Yes! Yes! Yes!" but she couldn't. Instead she cried out:

"I can't! I can't. I just can't."

With that Palmer hurriedly put her clothes on and bolted out of the door, leaving David mute.

Chapter Thirteen

Dave had nearly blurted out, "I know about your face, Palmer, and I know how much you must hurt, but I want you desperately! But he remained in stunned silence as the love of his life walked out of the door.

"Tomorrow," he thought, "I must confess that I've known all along." It was Dave's belief that Palmer's psyche was so damaged that she herself, should be the one to eventually break the news. However, now he wasn't so sure. Little did he know that tomorrow might not come. Meanwhile Palmer had rushed home to her mom and dad.

Palmer arrived at her parents' home and cried, "He asked me to marry him, mom! My heart is breaking."

"You knew this day would come, Palmer. I only wish I knew what to say or do, sweetheart. This is the only time in my life that I have no knowledge as to advise you. I know this, dear. You are the most beautiful daughter any mother has ever had. Whatever decisions you make, just know that dad and I are behind you 100%."

"I know that, mom, and I love you!"

"Just know this, dear. Perhaps the longer you wait, the more difficult it will be, and that goes for the both of you. David will eventually have to know. Covid-19 will not last forever…at least we hope not."

Palmer's "Bedtime Bunny Bee's" cabbage patch doll face required countless hours of surgery to reconstruct what was formerly her astonishingly beautiful countenance. Despite potent narcotics administered during the times that she was not undergoing actual surgery very often painful needle injections were part of her norm. These injections were preceded by numerous anesthetics which blocked nerve signals and therefore, reduced the pain during Palmer's invasive procedures. But her decision as how to inform Dave of her life-changing calamity hung over her in a suffocating manner.

Chapter Fourteen

It is often said that in each of our lives a moment arrives that forever changes it, dependent on the decision made by those included. That moment arrived unexpectedly as Palmer was walking to Dave's apartment to finally confront her tragically acquired visage. She was simply going to reveal to Dave what she now actually looked like, which was in her mind, "Bedtime Bunny Bee," a cabbage patch kid.

In fact, she had rehearsed the brief stage play in her mind.

"Hey, David, look! Voila! This is the woman you proposed marriage to!" Palmer was prepared for the worst. Get it done with. It's all over. No hard feelings. I understand this will not work for you. Please don't attempt to comfort me, I'm a big girl now. I'll just leave. Have a nice life.

Dave had called Palmer and asked if she would just come over and discuss their future together. He promised to not be overbearing or adamant and allow Palmer's heart to be the determining factor in her decisions. He knew that he indeed, had won her heart and was also aware that she had absolutely no clue that he knew of her disfiguration. Just as Palmer had planned, Dave was also going to "come clean" regarding his knowledge of her life-changing accident.

After crying for a full hour, Palmer put on some frumpy looking clothing attempting to appear even "plainer" looking than normal and took off on foot to confront her demons. All Palmer was armed with was her removable mask and what was left of her pride. It was on Marlborough Street in Boston's Back Bay where she saw the tall thin woman pushing a baby carriage. The woman was approximately fifty feet ahead of Palmer, but she turned around at the sound of Palmer's approaching footsteps. At once Palmer saw that the young woman's face had been horrifically burned, this despite the mask covering it.

Palmer saw the woman's charred lips, her reddish forehead, and the peeled skin around the young mother's ears. Palmer came to a full stop and suddenly asked if she could see the baby.

The young mother then sternly replied, "Don't worry, she doesn't look anything like me!"

Palmer took her words to be more than slightly sarcastic. It was as if she believed Palmer to be a voyeur or some sort of nasty person. It was then that Palmer Stevenson came to a complete stop and suddenly pulled down her own mask. Upon seeing Palmer's reconstructed face, her rebuilt nose and the tears welling in her eyes, she apologized:

"I'm so sorry, miss. But you know how people can be. I didn't know."

Palmer hesitated and responded softly, "It's all right. I understand."

Palmer leaned over and peered into the carriage.

"Your baby is beautiful. What's her name?"

"Her name is Amber. She'll be a year-old next month."

"May I ask your name?"

"My name is Felicia. And yours is?"

"I'm Palmer. I was in a horrific car accident. Lots of surgery."

"I'm so sorry. Mine was the result of a fire. They say it's a miracle I lived, and even more of a miracle my baby survived…Now sometimes I wish I hadn't"

"You were pregnant?"

"Yes, four months, but my fiancé, we never married, bailed out as soon as he saw my face."

Felicia paused to open her purse. Within moments she removed a photograph and showed it to Palmer. Felicia had been a beautiful redhead, but now she was simply red.

Palmer was surprised at how at ease she was in speaking with the young mother. The two young attractive women exchanged contact information. Upon embracing and sharing tears, the two burn victims

135

took off in opposite directions. Palmer had now reversed her course and decided to not continue with her journey to see David. Palmer reasoned it was better to not complete her trip, but to begin a new journey. It was better, she thought, to end her relationship with wonderful memories rather than add what was certain, she thought, to be heartbreak and sorrow.

Chapter Fifteen

Palmer Stevenson knew what she had to do, and she reacted distinctly and instantaneously. Immediately, she called her colleague and veterinary partner Dr. Vanessa Trembley and filled her in as to her plan. There was no way, she thought, that would provide her the sufficient emotional stability or fearlessness required to confront David with her "truth." Palmer was convinced that she could not sustain what she felt would be his negative and therefore, relationship ending reaction to learning Palmer was no longer the beautiful woman photographed with his dog.

Immediately after hanging up with Vanessa, Palmer telephoned Dave to apologize for having to cancel their evening together. Vanessa, although deeply concerned for Palmer's well-being, agreed to be complicit in what would be an enormous life-altering step.

"Are you sure, Palmer? This is a rather bold and sudden decision."

"I'm really certain, Vanessa. It's just that at this moment I don't have the courage to explain all of this to David, and I'm completely petrified of how he'd react if he saw me. I feel so guilty in leaving you alone with all of our clients, but I know you can handle it."

"Don't worry about me, Palmer. Just take care of yourself. When are you telling your mom and dad?"

"I'll tell them as quickly as I call David."

"Just be careful. We all love you!"

Palmer then immediately called David and informed him that a veterinary emergency had occurred and that she could not see him. However, she said, "I just want you to know that I've never loved anyone as much as I love you, and I want you to remember that!"

David, although slightly confused by Palmer's sudden change in demeanor and attitude, patted his dog and responded over the phone:

"I adore you, Palmer. When can I see you? We have so much to talk about."

"Very soon, David. I've got to go. There's an animal to save."

Palmer immediately went to see her parents. Although dismayed, they all cried, but promised Palmer they would not betray her. No matter how much David might ask, he was not to learn of her whereabouts or why she had left so abruptly.

Chapter Sixteen

Bar Harbor, Maine is one of the most desirable tourist locations in North America, but its remoteness prevents overcrowding. It's common for ships sailing from Europe to dock on its magnificent shoreline and Acadia National Park is heaven for those choosing beauty, hiking, bicycling or a combination of all. It is there that Dr. Palmer Stevenson chose to "hideout" for lack of a better description.

Within two months, Palmer had rented an apartment in nearby Southwest Harbor and leased a storefront in town to once more startup her veterinary practice. It was now early fall in New England, and a place where autumn arrived early rife with its spectacular foliage. Since Covid-19 had not yet been entirely vanquished, Palmer, as well as most of the residents in the area around Mt. Desert Island, continued to wear masks in public.

Palmer's ebullient personality and affable demeanor soon earned her numerous happy pet-owned customers, but Palmer seldom enjoyed any of Bar Harbor's many outstanding restaurants, rather than stop in for takeout food on occasion. Her mom and dad visited her once or twice, but the subject of David was never brought up. Albert and Marie Stevenson would leave that up to their beautiful daughter, that is, if she ever had the desire or inclination to discuss it.

Often at night, however, Palmer would think of David, wondering how he was, if he still loved her or perhaps had moved on to another young woman. "What ifs" haunted her waking hours on occasion, too, and she would sometimes wonder if she should have considered revealing her damaged features. That thought was nearly invariably followed by Palmer reasoning to herself, "How could he possibly still be attracted to a monster?" Obviously, Palmer was far from a monster.

David, of course, upon seeing that Palmer failed to return his calls, had arrived at the veterinary practice now run exclusively by Vanessa, the day following the alleged "medical emergency." David did not inform Vanessa that he was aware of what Palmer now looked like, but immediately ascertained that his love's colleague had been sworn to secrecy.

"David, I'm really sorry, but Palmer needed some time away to reassess her future, and she did not give me permission to tell anyone of her whereabouts or why she had departed. Just know this, David. She made it clear that there is no one else and that she loves you very much. That's all I can say."

"Is it possible to at least tell me where she is now located?"

"I will ask Palmer the next time she calls, but I believe she desperately wants solitude at this time. I have your number, David, and I promise to call you if anything changes. She did tell me that her greatest concern is your happiness."

"Vanessa, it's nearly impossible for me to be happy being away from Palmer. I adore her."

"I believe you, David, but it's apparently very complicated, but again, she stated unequivocally that there is no one else."

With that, David left and responded, "Please tell Palmer that I'll wait for her as long as it takes. She's worth waiting for."

The older woman, tears welling in her eyes, replied, "I know this, David. You have great taste in women, or in this case, one woman, that being Palmer Stevenson. And yes, I'll indeed, tell Palmer everything you said."

Chapter Seventeen

David waited for a brief period, but he could no longer risk losing Palmer forever. Therefore, he took a deep breath and concluded that to secure the love of his life a more drastic act must take place.

Dave Grace felt his heart beating in his throat as he arrived at the home of Albert and Marie Stevenson, the parents of beautiful Palmer. Of course, Palmer's parents fervently promised their daughter that they would never betray her by divulging her horrible accident which left her disfigured.

Upon seeing Dave arrive at their door, obviously they both were extremely surprised to see the outwardly worried young man standing forlornly at the entrance to their home.

Marie spoke first by saying, "Please come in, David. It's good to see you. Please sit down."

Dave decided to drop the bombshell immediately as he spoke softly, "Mr. and Mrs. Stevenson. I am so in love with Palmer that I cannot even think straight. Let me get this out of the way immediately. I've known about Palmer's tragic accident even before we met and the fact it disfigured her. I had no way of conveying what I had known from the start, and I was fearful of frightening her away and forever losing her."

Albert and Marie Stevenson both gasped and reached out to touch Dave's hand.

Dave then continued, "After she had literally saved the life of my beloved dog, I read the article in the Boston Globe describing the horrific events of that accident and I saw the "before and after" photographs of your still beautiful daughter. I also read that she was engaged to be married. Before I read the "engaged to be married" line I had already fallen madly in love with Palmer's AFTER countenance.

There was no pity for her whatsoever, just love at what she is regardless of her looks."

By this time Albert Stevenson was gulping and tears were welling in Marie Stevenson's eyes.

"I'm pretty much begging you, Mr. and Mrs. Stevenson. If you know where she is I must tell her how I feel."

The following morning, Dave climbed behind the wheel and with his dog Reggie he began to make the trip of his lifetime to Bar Harbor, Maine.

Upon visiting Palmer's veterinary practice that afternoon, he was told by an assistant that Palmer was most likely sitting on her favorite bench near Sand Beach in Acadia National Park. That is where he found her, but more accurately where Reggie the labrador retriever found her.

Palmer was comfortably seated on a bench and reading a book. She was wearing a mask.

Reggie startled her by nuzzling her.

"Oh, my God! Reggie!"

Standing behind Reggie, of course, was David, his heart in his hands.

"Palmer, I cannot live without you. You are the love of my life. I want to grow old and wrinkled and funny looking with you!"

'David," sobbed Palmer, her eyes welling with tears, "there's something you don't know about me, and I fear that knowledge would change the way you feel about our future, but I do want you to know that I love you with all my heart."

Dave gently dried her tears with his handkerchief and softly replied, "Palmer, my love. I've known about your accident, your numerous surgeries, the pain you've endured, and I've seen you with your mask off. I read the piece in the Boston Globe, the one that showed the before and after photographs. I immediately fell in love with the "after." You're perfect, angel. I need you!"

What Lies Beneath

Three years have passed since that fateful encounter in Bar Harbor's Acadia National Park. Dave and Palmer Grace. The perfect couple with a baby boy and a baby girl.

The best "man" at their wedding was Reggie, a still vibrant golden retriever.

WHEN TOMORROW
BECOMES YESTERDAY

For Jen-Bricker-Bauer

Dominic Bauer, Jen Bricker-Bauer, and Scott and Peggy Russell

When He calls his angels home, you'll know our time here on Earth is done.

— Scott D. Russell

Never travel faster than your guardian angel can fly.

— Mother Teresa

Preface

This tale is about abandonment. Abandonment of compassion. Abandonment of harmony. Abandonment of ideals. Abandonment of caring. Abandonment of civility. Abandonment of humanity. Abandonment of each other, and ultimately, the abandonment of our species.

At the tail end of this story, I will reveal myself. Please keep a mirror within reach.

When Tomorrow Becomes Yesterday

Chapter One

The warning sign at Ogunquit Beach in the beautiful town of Ogunquit, Maine, could very well have served as a metaphor for the life of sixteen-year-old Adalyn Robertson. As the beautiful girl approached the sand below the ramp leading down to the beach overlooking the Atlantic Ocean, she came upon the sign which read, "Swim at Your Own Risk. No Lifeguard on Duty."

The year was 2016, and Adalyn was in her junior year of high school in Roxbury, Massachusetts, a predominantly African American enclave of Boston. Adalyn was with her mom, Barbara, and was about to inform her mother of a dream she wished to pursue, but she was hesitant to tell her mom for a myriad of reasons, the foremost being the cost involved in seeking such an endeavor. Adalyn and her mom walked down the beach towards a row of houses in Moody, Maine, just south of Wells, when Adalyn drew a deep breath on the unseasonably cool early summer day. Upon reaching one of the bridges that abut the beach, Adalyn finally worked up enough courage to say softly, "Mom, I've thought about this a lot, but I want to study nursing in college. I truly want to devote my life to helping people and doing something useful for society."

Adalyn understood that finances were tight, especially when considering that her mom was a single mother. Barbara was the head of the household and her job as an accountant for a law firm in Boston could only go so far in supporting her beautiful daughter and her three sons, Reggie, who had died tragically at 18, Stephen, 17, and William,

14. Therefore, it surprised Adalyn when her mom smiled and answered, "Then, a nurse you will be! We'll make it work. Your dad would've been so proud!"

Adalyn's father, Eric, had been killed in action in Afghanistan in 2014 when she was sixteen years-old, leaving Barbara a widow with their three children. Within two years of his father's death, Reggie, the oldest boy, was shot and killed by a police officer in Mattapan, Massachusetts. The benefits Barbara received from Eric's military service, helped in paying some bills, but raising three teenagers in the inner city with a limited income and the inherent existent dangers were not an easy task for the young widow. However, Barbara's only daughter desired to be a nurse, and she wasn't about to interfere with her dream.

Sergeant Eric Robertson, whose late father Bertram, had also proudly served in the military, was a mere thirty-six years old when he was killed by a mortar attack by Islamic extremists, and the result of his death had a devastating effect on his young family. All three boys, and of course, Adalyn, adored their father.

After returning to the spot where Adalyn and her mom had entered onto the beach, Adalyn once more peered at the sign which listed the "flag system" which read in English and French as follows:

Green – (Vert) – Safe
Blue – (Bleu) – Swim with Caution
Red – (Rouge) – Swim at Your Own Risk

Beautiful Adalyn was about to enter a brand new and foreign world and the bright youngster would thrust herself into it without even a hint of trepidation. She was her father's daughter.

As for Reggie, he began to drift nearly immediately after his father's death in Iraq. Normally a good student, he lapsed into an untrusting youth, and one who invariably questioned authority including his teachers. Reggie began to skip classes and hang out with some of the numerous gang members in his community. What good was the military to minorities, he spewed to all that would listen. What good did it do for his dad? Did our country or our political leaders give a rat's ass about the poor people in our inner cities? Reggie was bitter, and perhaps rightfully so.

Chapter Two

It was evident early on that Adalyn Robertson was stunningly attractive. Her sharp facial features, her black curly reddish hair, her bright smile, and her ebullient personality was palpable. When combined with her glowing skin, she radiated beauty as she had the complexion of an Ethiopian princess. However, having had an older brother named Reggie too often elicited whispers and many made assumptions that her pedigree, so to speak, might include a few of Reggie's undesirable traits. Adalyn's road was therefore paved with additional obstacles, but Adalyn would not be denied her dream of becoming a nurse and better. In both school and the workplace, there was always the albatross named Reggie, but Adalyn remained steadfast in her pursuit of her lofty goal, and she won over her teachers and supervisors with her personality and enduring spirit.

Beautiful Adalyn graduated from Simmons College with honors in 2019 and immediately attained a job as a nurse at Brigham & Women's Hospital in Boston. She was a mere 21 years of age, but already had made a significant mark for herself at the hospital and was beloved by both her doctors and colleagues and entire staff at the prestigious institution. And then the specter of dreaded Covid suddenly hung like a shroud over our entire planet. The virus, whose origins are still debated to this day, adversely affected hospitals, hospital employees, patients, and taxed all on the front lines of the battle, and a war it was and is. Doctors, nurses, technicians, researchers and all first responders were particularly thrust into the front lines of the struggle. Hospital rooms were scarce, tens of thousands of hospital staffs had contracted the virus, and so many staff members had to literally do the work of the physicians who had come down with the plague. Adalyn, therefore, was front and center in the massive struggle. She did so willingly and courageously and without blinking an eyelash.

Adalyn, as so many of her fellow associates did, toiled nearly around the clock, sometimes sleeping on the floor of the hospital with makeshift sleeping quarters. There was a battle to be won, a battle we could not lose, a battle for life itself. Despite being emotionally and physically exhausted, Adalyn and her team of nurses, knew that this was a war that could not be lost under any circumstances.

One of Adalyn's patients was a beautiful blonde twenty-six-year-old Caucasian woman named Jordan Cosgrove. She was a mother of two young children, a boy, James, Jr., six years-old, and a girl, four-year-old Madison. Her husband, James, Sr., also twenty-six, was not permitted to even visit his ill wife, who had come down with Covid. Hospital regulations and other protocol restrictions and strict mandates had been put in place to prevent the spreading of the deadly virus.

As Jordan's condition worsened, her husband James' emotional status deteriorated commensurately. He was now permitted to view his suffering wife through a plate glass window, and he grew increasingly morose and sullen as a feeling of helplessness overwhelmed him, not being able to even comfort his ailing wife by even holding her hand. Upon returning home to care for his two young children, he had absolutely no idea as to how to comfort himself, let along the kids who were being tended to by his mom or mother-in-law most of the time. Adalyn witnessed first-hand the devastating effect it had on James, and she desperately wanted to comfort him, but had no opportunity to do so, since she was now responsible for countless other Covid sufferers in the hospital. At one time, James had shown Adalyn photographs of the kids and the young couple in happier and healthier times, and it tugged at her heartstrings. As courageous as Adalyn was, she too, was powerless in her helplessness.

The bravery of these first responders was beyond anything imaginable.

Chapter Three

Several years before the horrific pandemic, a young man named Ramesh Gupta, in search of a better world, relocated his young family from Gujarat in India to the United States. Ramesh, along with wife, Shirisha and their two small children, settled in the inner city of Boston, Massachusetts, where Ramesh became a cherished member of his community, which was comprised of mostly minorities. Long before the pandemic, which accentuated the wide chasm between the haves and the have-nots, Ramesh Gupta's benevolence in his neighborhood was noted and appreciated by the residents he often offered credit to during hardships. Ramesh's own father had been killed by members of the Chinese army in a border skirmish.

It was Ramesh's humanity that Ramesh's wife, Shirisha, fell in love with before the couple moved to the U.S. Ramesh, from the state of Gujarat on the western coast of India, which lies on the Kathiawar peninsula, with a massive population of 60.4 million people, is bounded primarily by Pakistan to the north, Madhya Pradesh to the east, and Maharashta to the southwest, was a far cry from Mattapan in Boston.

Shirisha, on the other hand, hailed from Nepal, and they had met in Bombay at a health convention. Their young children were Aalam, a boy, and Ajay, a girl. They doted on their kids but were strict in insisting they become devout students and receive good educations.

Upon settling in an apartment in Mattapan, Ramesh purchased a convenience store and quickly became a respected and beloved part of his community. His compassion for those less fortunate was palpable. Despite the inherent dangers which included many young gang members in his neighborhood, Ramesh saw no need to even carry any sort of weapon when running his establishment. The residents of the area knew he'd take care of them in their times of need.

Then one hot sweltering evening in mid-summer, two young thugs entered the convenience store, and one youth brandished a pistol and pointed it at Ramesh and demanded he empty his cash register. The lone defense Ramesh had at his disposal was the button beneath his counter, a device which would alert the local police station, a mere two blocks away.

As Ramesh told the two youthful thieves to calm down, and that he'd hand them the money in his register, one of the robbers noticed that Ramesh had reached beneath the counter to alert the police. The robber shouted, "Look out! He's got a gun!" With that, the other youth shot Ramesh in the chest.

All Ramesh had done was attempt to push the button to alert the nearby local police precinct within yards of the store. Ramesh, while falling to the ground managed to push the button. The police arrived within two minutes, but one of the youths remained and began grabbing several food items off the shelves.

The police arrived at the precise time that the mortally wounded Ramesh Gupta had staggered out into the street. "They shot me!" Ramesh cried, as he pointed to the two assailants.

"Stop or I'll shoot!" shouted one of the two responding police officers. However, the youth with the gun, turned and aimed the weapon at the officer. The police officer immediately fired at the robber, killing him instantly. The youth and Ramesh died just a few yards from each other in the streets of Mattapan. Four months after Ramesh Gupta's brutal and senseless murder, Shirisha gave birth to her third child, a little girl, Adweta, who entered the world without her father, and beautiful Adalyn faced the future without her older brother, Reggie, who had been killed by a police officer's gun in the unforgiving streets of Mattapan.

Chapter Four

As Covid continued to ravage Jordan Cosgrove's once healthful body, Adalyn Robertson remained her conduit to the outside world, and of course, the lone pipeline capable of communicating messages to her beloved husband, James, and their two frightened children. As often as she could, Adalyn would sit at Jordan's bedside, gently holding her hand and repeating the loving words from James, and on several occasions, messages of hope and love from their two children, James, Jr., and Madison. Then one day, an emotionally exhausted Adalyn heard the words she had feared for so long. Suddenly awakening from one of her lengthy slumbers while on her life-saving ventilator, Jordan Cosgrove opened her eyes and motioned for Adalyn to come closer.

As Adalyn reached for Jordan's hand, the deathly ill young mother pleaded, "I know you've been here for me all along even when I cannot respond. Just know that I love you, but there is something you must know. I know in my heart I'm not going to make it. My time is short here on Earth. Please promise me something."

As tears welled in Adalyn's eyes, the beautiful young nurse answered, "Anything. I promise I'll do anything for you, but please, don't give up, Jordan. Have faith. Please tell me what you want."

"Please promise me, Adalyn, that you'll take care of James for me. He won't make it without me. And please take care of my kids, Jimmy, and Madison. Only you can do it."

A shocked Adalyn hadn't a clue as to how to respond to Jordan Cosgrove's plea. But rather than ask how she could possibly fulfill such an enormously improbable task, Adalyn, while choking back her tears was surprised upon hearing her own words, "I promise I will, Jordan. I'll do everything humanly possible."

What Lies Beneath

Jordan Cosgrove, her lungs filled with fluids, died within two days of her prayer, leaving Adalyn Robertson pressured and bewildered beyond comprehension about how to fulfill the enormous responsibility bequeathed upon her.

Chapter Five

Immediately following the death of Jordan Cosgrove, Adalyn's immediate supervisor, Nancy Furst, along with Adam Lucien, the Chief Administrator of the hospital, told Adalyn Robertson to take at least two days off. Both superiors considered Adalyn a huge part of the future of Brigham & Women's Hospital, and were completely cognizant of her abilities, professionalism, and genuine compassion for others, but most of all her dedication to her craft and her patients and fellow staff members. They were also aware that Adalyn was working herself into an unremitting exhaustion, both physically and mentally.

"There is a significantly important position for you, Adalyn, at this institution, and it is not in the too distant future. You are beyond special. Now go home and get some needed rest. Both fatigue and the exposure to this dreaded virus put you at a much greater risk. Therefore, we insist you get some quality rest. You are much too important to lose." advised Dr. Adam Lucien, the chief of the hospital.

The death of Jordan Cosgrove was difficult enough for Adelyn to endure, but seeing her husband, James completely crumble and go to pieces had already placed beautiful Adalyn in a nearly delirious state, but the dying Jordan's desperate plea managed to place her in what was most certainly an untenable situation. Adalyn had been given the keys to a universe she was not familiar with. Here! Save my family! Save our lives!

But Adalyn was the son of her father, the war hero who had given his life in Iraq for his beloved country. Like her dad, Adalyn decided to react with all her resources, no matter the cost.

Chapter Six

W hen you are Adalyn Robertson, aka Florence Nightengale, there are no days off. There are lives to be saved, regardless of pandemics, earthquakes, tornados and floods and pestilence. There are angels among us, and ravishing Adalyn most definitely was the embodiment of that stature. However, the young dying woman's request seemed so implausible, so biblical in its ramifications, that even someone imbued with the spirit, faith and mindset of young Adalyn was rendered incapable of even having the slightest inkling of how to deal with what seemed virtually impossible.

Therefore, on Adalyn's initial "day off" in nearly two months, she dressed quietly and planned to visit the widow, James Cosgrove. As Adalyn drove to his home in Newton, Massachusetts, she literally had no idea of what she would say to him, and certainly not to his two now motherless young children. Adalyn, carrying a bouquet of flowers, took a deep breath, placed a mask over her nose and mouth, and prepared to visit the devastated family. Jordan Cosgrove had given her an oath, one of course, impossible to fulfill.

Adalyn rang the doorbell and waited for perhaps thirty seconds, a time which equated to an eternity in the nurse's mind. The door opened, but James Cosgrove, Sr. was not present to answer it. Adalyn was slightly surprised to see a lovely middle-aged woman standing inside. The woman introduced herself as James' mother, Adele.

"Hi, sorry to intrude during your time of grief. My name is Adalyn Robertson. I had the honor and privilege of caring for your beautiful daughter-in-law, Jordan, during the time she courageously battled the dreaded virus, Adele. I'm so sorry we could not save her. Her loss, although one of thousands, was so devastating to all of us. I cannot even imagine...." Adalyn's words ceased as she immediately became teary-eyed and choked up.

"Please come inside, Adalyn. Both my son and Jordan spoke so highly of you. You are a saint."

Within moments, Adele Cosgrove led Adalyn to a sofa where she motioned her to be seated. Adele then said softly, "My son is having a simply awful time in accepting that Jordan is gone. He is staying with friends at this moment. I am taking care of both James, Jr., and Madison. The kids are devastated, of course. This is an impossible situation for all of us. Their virtual home-schooling is now a complete disaster. I am widowed as well. My grandchildren cry all the time. I try, but I've had so little success in comforting them. They loved Jordan so much."

Adalyn was not about to tell Adele Cosgrove of her daughter-in-law's dying plea. There was enough heartbreak without adding to the already horrific scenario.

Before leaving, Adele admitted to Adalyn that her son seemed to be in dire straits. "I'm truly frightened for him. He seems to be entirely vacant. He's vulnerable currently. I can see this becoming a serious issue. I plan to take care of little Jimmy and Madison for as long as it takes. James is my son, but I'm really frightened. Perhaps you can speak with him."

Adalyn took down the contact information and informed Adele that she'd attempt to see him. Adele then sadly admitted, "James is not staying with friends, as I had said. He wanted to be entirely alone for a short while. He's staying at this hotel in Brookline."

At that moment, the two kids, James, Jr., and Madison peeked out from a bedroom. They both appeared to be forlorn and had the countenance of children who had just lost their beloved mother, which, of course, they had.

Adalyn Robertson asked the youngsters if she could possibly join them in their bedroom. Both kids shrugged their shoulders as if to convey, what difference would it make. Adalyn sat on the floor with them for well over an hour, and by the time she left, she managed to elicit a few smiles and even a few laughs from the kids. Madison was taken by the ebullient African American beauty.

"Can you come back?" asked Madison, the spitting image of her mom.

"Anytime that I can," answered Adalyn. "I promise."

Meanwhile, James Jr., briefly smiled through the tears welling in his eyes, but asked, "Where's my daddy?"

As Adele Cosgrove led Adalyn to the door, she asked if the young nurse would perhaps briefly lower her mask.

"We're all vaccinated," said Adele, "I just want to see what you really look like."

Otherworldly beautiful Adalyn Robertson, nurse extraordinaire, lowered her mask and smiled. Adele Cosgrove and Adalyn embraced. The hug lasted a full minute.

"Oh my God!" Adele exclaimed, "gosh, you're so pretty!"

Adalyn teared up as she was leaving. She planned on visiting the widow, James, Sr., in the morning, her second scheduled "day off." Again, she had no idea of what to say to him.

Chapter Seven

On Sunday morning, Adalyn awoke and showered and dressed, and planned to visit James Cosgrove, the young widow. She peered at the address provided to her by Adele Cosgrove, a motel just off Commonwealth Avenue in Brookline. After parking her car in the lot, Adalyn donned her mask and took off in search of Room 107, the room James had booked.

Upon knocking on the door, Adalyn received no response, but then noticed that the door was apparently slightly ajar. Adalyn then inquired, "James? Are you here?" There was still no answer, so Adalyn opened the door slowly and entered cautiously. It was 10:00 AM, but she quickly realized that James was still in bed. Adalyn softly then asked, "James, are you awake?"

After receiving no response, Adalyn opened the curtains to allow light to enter the darkened room and immediately arrived at the conclusion that something was amiss. James lay motionless in bed and seemed entirely unaware that the young nurse had entered his living quarters. Adalyn, although a mere youngster herself, immediately sprung into action.

Adalyn rushed into the bathroom, and immediately spotted the empty bottle of pills on the sink. "Barbiturates!" Adalyn cried out. She hurriedly sprinted back to where James was virtually unconscious and began to shake him.

"You stupid fool! You jackass!" Adalyn shouted. "Your kids need you!"

Adalyn began slapping James Cosgrove in the face and shaking him with all the strength she had in her 5' 2" 105 lb. frame. "You fool! You damned fool!"

James began to emerge from his drug induced and life-threatening stupor. He quickly realized that Adalyn, his conduit to his late beloved wife, was the one attempting to revive him.

"What are you doing here, Nurse Robertson? How did you find me?"

"You damned fool! shouted Adalyn, "your children need you. What would killing yourself do for them?"

James immediately went into denial:

"I'm not trying to kill myself. I just took some sleeping pills."

"Don't lie to me!" shouted Adalyn. "I'm a nurse, and I'm from Mattapan! Do you think I don't know what you did here?! This type of crap is all over our streets!"

Adalyn thrust the empty bottle of barbiturates in front of James' now guilty face. "They cloud your thinking. These are addictive! You don't have a prescription for these, do you?! You don't suffer from anxiety or insomnia or have a seizure disorder, do you?! These are addictive, you fool! You could have killed yourself! Where did you get these?"

"Listen, Adalyn. My life is over. I cannot go on without Jordan. I don't want to live."

Adalyn was now furious as she spewed, "You don't want to live? Your kids need you! They love you! I made a promise to Jordan. I am going to keep it, damn you!"

James swallowed hard and asked, "What promise did you make?"

Adalyn signed deeply and answered, "That's between Jordan, me and God. Now you must tell me where you got these drugs, and you better not lie to me. I'm not kidding."

Adalyn took down the information James provided to her. Then James finally sat up and thanked Adalyn for her intervention.

"You can go now, Adalyn. Seriously, thanks for the reality check."

Adalyn lowered her mask and replied softly but sternly, "I'm not going anywhere. I'm taking you home! Now take a shower and get dressed!"

After stopping at a Dunkin Donuts for a significant dose of coffee, Adalyn ushered James into his home in Newton, where his children, James, Jr., and Madison rushed into his arms.

"Daddy, where have you been?" Both children then hugged Adalyn unabashedly, while Adele Cosgrove looked on in amazement at what the young nurse had achieved. "I cannot thank you enough." said James.

"Will you come back to visit us?" asked Madison, as Jimmy looked on plaintively.

"Yes," replied Adalyn, who had most likely just saved the life of the young widow, "but only if your daddy approves."

"I strongly approve," answered James.

Adalyn hugged the kids and left, but not before thoroughly checking James' medicine cabinets. Adalyn re-emerged and as she left, she told the children, "I have to go back to work tomorrow. There are patients I must tend to. But I promise to see you soon."

Chapter Eight

If James Cosgrove was really attempting to end his life, he had fortunately botched it. Despite doing an enormously large amount of research regarding James' past, Adalyn was now convinced that his bout with depression, which, of course, was not over, was no longer a life-threatening situation. Both Adalyn and Adele, his mom, had thoroughly convinced him that his children needed him desperately, especially at the most formative period of their young lives. Life without their beloved mom, Jordan, was daunting enough, and James would not suffer a relapse into thoughts of suicide.

Despite the specter of Covid and the resulting pandemic hanging like a shroud over the planet, things were indeed improving, and significant research and vaccines offered hope that a brighter future appeared on the horizon.

Adalyn would indeed visit James and the kids on occasion, but the thought that her pledge to Jordan that she'd be their savior no longer haunted Adalyn's dreams. This even though it was obvious that she found James extremely attractive and that both little Jimmy and Madison absolutely worshiped her.

One evening in the fall of the year of Covid, James invited Adalyn out for dinner in Boston's South End, and they shared laughter and wine. What Adalyn was not aware of was that Jimmy and Madison had asked their father why he didn't marry Adalyn, whom of course, they adored. The children's remark caught James completely off guard, and he had no retort, since he had never thought of such a possibility despite finding Adalyn both wonderful and sexually attractive.

After sharing a superb dinner together, James drove Adalyn back to her apartment in Mattapan. James was preparing to leave when Adalyn invited him in for a while. James accepted, but was surprised, or perhaps shocked, when he suddenly took Adalyn in his arms and kissed her. He immediately apologized, however, with, "I'm so sorry. That was entirely out of character, Adalyn. It won't happen again."

Adalyn reacted by saying, "You mean, you didn't intend to kiss me?"

James, slightly embarrassed, replied, "You're a complete lady. I'm sorry if I offended you."

With that, Adalyn smiled and took James by the shoulders and kissed him tenderly.

"I love you, and I love your kids, James. There is nothing to apologize for."

"I never told you this, Adalyn, but you're gorgeous. I really do adore you."

Within minutes, James and Adalyn made love for the first time. They used zero protection. For both, this was a first, both being strict about such protocol. Adalyn, the young astoundingly great nurse, was no longer just "married to her job."

At one point after the lovemaking, James blurted out, "I feel as if I cheated on Jordan."

Adalyn, of course, had no clue as to how to respond.

Chapter Nine

After not hearing from Adalyn for several weeks, James became increasingly worried. Therefore, he called her at home one evening and asked if anything was wrong.

"James," replied Adalyn, "it's not your fault, but I'm pregnant." She hesitated before continuing, "with your child. It's all right, though. I will get an abortion."

"Don't be absurd, Adalyn. I love you with all my heart. I want to marry you immediately! The kids love you, too. They want you desperately! And so do I!"

Adalyn Robertson, the absurdly beautiful young nurse, was about to improbably fulfill the dying wishes of Jordan Cosgrove. A bright future finally appeared on the vista, but like everything else during these perilous times, dark clouds were about to appear on the horizon.

Chapter Ten

Adalyn's mom, Barbara, reacted with a reserved joyfulness. "Being a black woman with a white widowed husband with their two children can present some serious obstacles, but you've overcome all barriers in the past, my love, and this too, will end in victory! I'm a bit surprised that you're pregnant, though, but this just seems right to me. Congratulations, Adalyn. Your dad, Eric, would have scolded you, but he loved you dearly, too!"

Upon informing her two brothers Stephen and William, however, things were about to get rocky.

"A white dude with kids? You're kidding me, right? And you're pregnant, sis?" exclaimed Stephen the older of the two siblings. "You do remember that some white cop killed Reggie, right?"

"You can't go on hating everyone, Stephen. There are good and bad people of all colors," replied Adalyn.

"Bullshit!" answered Stephen. Dad died for this country, remember. What good came of that? What's the dude's name, anyhow?"

"His name is James Cosgrove, and he's a good man and a great father," Adalyn replied.

"Cosgrove?" Stephen Robertson replied. "Why does that name sound familiar?"

Stephen left the room for a few minutes and returned livid. "Cosgrove?! Look at this!"

In Stephen Cosgrove's hand was a newspaper article about the death of his brother, Reggie.

"Look at this, sis! This James Cosgrove motherfucker who just knocked you up is the younger brother of the cop who killed Reggie! His brother murdered Reggie and you're going to marry the motherfucker because he raped you! No, sis! I won't allow it!"

"Watch your mouth, Stephen!" scolded Barbara, "Reggie shot and killed that poor Indian shopkeeper in his convenience store. You know that in your heart. Everyone around here loved Ramesh! Reggie was my son, my flesh and blood. I brought him into this world. What was that policeman supposed to do?"

"You weren't there, mom. You didn't see it! How do you know what happened?"

"Enough!" shouted Barbara, the widow of a combat hero, "I'll not tolerate that type of behavior in my home!"

With that, Stephen Robertson hurriedly ran out of the apartment and slammed the door behind him.

Chapter Eleven

There is no "Chapter Eleven." Please read the postscript.

Postscript

According to Wikipedia, "Chapter Eleven," which does not as YET appear in this book, is defined as follows:

"Chapter 11 of the United States Bankruptcy Code (Title 11 of the United States Code) permits reorganization under the bankruptcy laws of the United States. Such reorganization, known as "Chapter 11 bankruptcy", is available to every business, whether organized as a corporation, partnership or sole proprietorship, and to individuals, although it is most prominently used by corporate entities.

Bankruptcy, indeed. It is my belief that our species is nearly morally bankrupt, bereft of compassion and in serious endangerment. Therefore, I did not write "Chapter Eleven." You see, I have absolutely no inkling whatsoever of how my own story will end. I could have penned a syrupy conclusion, of how beautiful Adalyn's estranged brother apologized to his sister, attended her wedding to James and that all lived happily ever after. Or perhaps I could have employed the modern-day method of heartbreak and violence and told of still another family hopelessly fractured by hatred and fear. It is not my call.

I mentioned in the preface that I would reveal myself. Well, here it is: I am you.

How many of you secretly longed to write the "Great American Novel?" Well, this is your chance, finally. You see, the ending to this story will be written by you, dear reader.

I would like to believe, however, that the ending to this story will be told by our children, grandchildren, and great grandchildren. Perhaps it will be written by Adalyn and James' unborn baby, along with her two recently "adopted" children. Maybe there will be countless other chapters written. It is our only hope.

About the Author

Scott Russell was born and raised in the tenements of the South Bronx in his native New York. He remains deeply emotionally affected by the events of 9/11 and to this moment is incapable of visiting the site of the catastrophe, thus his stunningly powerful *Prophet's End*, the tome you are holding in your hands.

Scott is also the author of *The Scorekeeper*, *Joey*, and collaborated with the eccentric former major league baseball legend Bill "Spaceman" Lee on *The Spaceman Chronicles* and *The Final Odyssey of the Sweet Ride - Spaceman Lee's Epic Journey Across America*.

Scott currently resides in North Attleboro, Massachusetts with Peggy, his bride of 40 years and their assorted felines.